DARK CITY

-The Order of Shadows-

Book One

by Kit Hallows

DARK CITY

- The Order of Shadows -

Book One

Interior design by Kit Hallows

www.kithallows.com

Give feedback on the book at:
kit@kithallows.com

Twitter: @KitHallows

Second Edition

Printed in the U.S.A

To FFFF, Matt, Mr. Cat, & my readers, thank you

-ONE-

Bury Street was riddled with death. Its houses were long-abandoned empty husks, their shattered windows reflected the broken moon in web-like cracks while weeds sprung from gaps in the sidewalk and choked the wild flowers swaying in the dilapidated gardens. The only cars left in the street were propped up on cinder blocks, their windscreens smashed, the fragments glittering on the pavement like spilled jewels.

The families that had lived here were long gone. Foreclosures and evictions mainly, but shakedowns and violence quickly drove away any holdouts. Now it was like a ghost town.

All in all, the perfect place for my quarry to ply his grim trade.

The Organization hadn't supplied an exact address, just a street, but that was good enough for me. I reached into my battered leather bag and pulled out a pair of brass-rimmed glasses. The lenses, ground from thin pieces of magically charged crystal, granted me a temporary gift of enhanced sight. Usually I'd see thumping hearts, dim glowing lumps of meat pulsing in darkness, but my quarry had no heart. My quarry was dead.

Or should I say, *undead.*

A cool breeze swept through my hair as I glanced down the long row of dark houses.

And then I saw it, a glint of blood-red light.

A dying heart.

His victim.

I pulled the glasses off and waited for the world to reassemble itself. The heartbeat was situated somewhere in the upper part of a house at the end of the street. It was a nondescript building, its windows boarded with plywood, the paintwork cracked and peeled. The front door, a warped rectangle of graffitied wood.

It was hard to imagine the place had ever seen a happy day, but the rusted bicycle in the tangled clumps of ragweed might have told a different story.

Light flickered between the cracks of the boarded upstairs window and muffled music drifted down, faint but clear. Jazz, recorded by people long gone from our world.

It was an unnerving sound, a joyous clatter and racket in this place of pain. Celebratory almost.

I glanced up at the moon as if she might bring me luck, but there was no blessing from that full scarlet orb tonight.

The garden gate creaked as I pushed it open, like a sound effect from a vintage horror movie. I paused before the front door and checked my gun was loaded.

And then I heard it. A faint, strangled whimper.

A plea.

She was still alive.

For now at least.

I ran my hand across the rough wooden door until I reached the lock. The shard of crystal around my neck still held enough magic for what I needed. I closed my eyes and focused as I visualized the deadbolts rusting to brown and red dust.

I pushed the door and it swung open.

I switched my flashlight on and swept it over the threshold to the sprawling pile of circulars and take-out menus that had piled up beneath the mail slot. Damp discolorations on the putrid yellow wallpaper gave testimony to the furniture that had once been there. Aside from that, the hall was empty. No obvious traps.

A gleam of light twinkled from the landing of the second floor. The staircase was carpeted, a lucky break, providing my quarry was adequately distracted.

Another whelp rose over the music as it changed to a jaunty, brassy refrain, the mood totally at odds with the suffering whimpers. They were painful to hear but at least they meant he hadn't started feeding yet.

Because if he had, there'd have been no sounds at all. Still, my blood, already hot on this balmy September night, was beginning to boil lava-hot with rage.

I hated vampires. At least the unreformed ones. There was plenty of technology to assuage their need for human blood but some seemed to have a hard time changing old habits and instincts. While others yearned for the thrill of the chase, the bedazzlement of seduction, and the pulse of the vein. Others like my quarry, Mr. Tudor. But his lust for suffering was coming to an end, along with the trail of corpses he'd left across the city.

At first, distinguishing his handiwork amongst all of the other corpses piling up of late, had been a challenge. Death had hit the city hard. Cases were extreme and they got bloodier and bloodier as the summer progressed. The fine line dividing the magical and non-magical worlds seemed to be thinner than ever, and monstrous creatures like Tudor grew bolder by the day.

No one was safe, not even those with ties to The Organization. Which is why I'd told myself that this would be the last job. No more commissions, I had to get out of this dark game, just like I'd promised the woman I'd loved. And I would. Just as soon as I found the murderous bitch who had killed her.

But first, Tudor.

I moved carefully as I made my way up the stairs, but not cautiously enough. A trigger snapped below my foot as I reached the third step and I heard a wet, slithering sound. Like a slug slaking off its skin.

A heavy metallic and aniseed scent filled the air. An illusion trap. I clamped my coat sleeve over my mouth.

Too late.

The staircase shook and trembled as if the planet was turning in on itself. I flinched as the yellow wallpaper writhed and crawled like a living mosaic of millions of yellow ants. I dug into my bag for a means to break the spell and recoiled.

It felt like I'd plunged my hand into a corpse.

A burnt smell of soot seared my nostrils and my head swam. I glanced upstairs, expecting to find the beast descending, claws raised, ready to strike a killing blow as I squirmed in this half-paralyzed state.

But the staircase was empty.

The world heaved again and sent me spinning out of the here-and-now, to a place in the past I'd long since chosen to forget.

To the place I was born, aged ten. The asylum on the hill.

The walls turned from yellow to grey and a familiar stench pricked my nostrils; industrial disinfectants, shit and madness. Ancient screams echoed from the dilapidated corridor that appeared at the foot of the stairs, and a long shadow flickered below the fizzing fluorescent lights.

I stifled my cry as the stairway transformed into a line of black, brittle teeth and the carpet undulated like a tongue. I yelped as I grabbed the sizzling hot handrail and checked my palm for livid red marks, but it was clean.

"It's not real. None of it's real." It was my voice, but muffled. Like it was coming from an old chest in an attic in some other dimension. "Keep it together."

I took a breath that went nowhere and tried to gasp for another as the edges of the world dimmed and darkened. The whole universe seemed to shake and contract and suddenly I was propelled from my body and as I looked down I saw myself below the stairs. Nothing more than a boy.

Someone was leading me away, their hand in mine. I tried to see who it was, but their face was pixilated and blurred.

I froze as I descended toward the specter of my past self. Something brushed my corporeal throat and then I felt the rake of razor sharp nails as they punctured my flesh. This, along with the muffled whimper from Tudor's victim was enough to break the spell and draw my perception back to the present.

The asylum vanished and I found myself on the stairway with my head wedged against the yellow wall. Pain exploded through my neck as fingernails tore into the side of my throat.

-TWO-

I forced myself to remain perfectly still as the nails raked my flesh because as far as my attacker was concerned, I was somewhere else altogether. Locked in the illusions of his magical trap.

He moved around to face me. I stared ahead, looking past his eyes as if I was still lost in the terrible, dead black dream.

It was a vampire, but not the one I was looking for. This one hadn't fully turned yet. There was still a crazed thrill of excitement in his pinprick pupils, and his face hadn't yet taken on the lines and cracks of the fully initiated. He'd been a man once, and not long ago. Young, with a hipster mustache and pseudo Victorian clothes that served to make his appearance all the more grotesque.

He giggled as he tapped his nail on my jugular, ignoring the blood that trickled down toward my collarbone.

A wail came from the room at the top of the stairs, this time the sound was agonized.

It was feeding time at the zoo.

I whirled round and grabbed the vampire by the throat, my grip tight enough to silence him. His head was horribly malformed, his skin almost translucent, his eyes milky blue.

He bared his needle-like teeth and grimaced as I pulled my fist back and punched him hard in the side of the face.

Bone shattered beneath his skin.

I shoved him away. He tumbled down the stairs, his head striking the floorboards below with a horrible crack. He lay slumped by the doorway as I leapt down and twisted his head until his neck snapped. The light in his undead eyes dimmed as one foul, final breath wheezed through his lips.

A fresh wave of nausea passed through me, a side effect from the magical trap. I reached into my bag, grabbed a vial of Clariberry and pulled the cork free with my teeth. It smelled like rotting seaweed and burned my throat like cheap whiskey, but within moments the serum cleared the toxic spell from my mind.

I was back in the present and my past was back where it belonged; buried beneath a rock at the bottom of an endless well.

My heart raced as I climbed the stairs, watching for the telltale glint of magical traps. I found one hidden near the top step and cleared it as I leapt up into the hallway.

The short murky corridor ended in a wash of light that flickered as a shadow crossed it. The music roared with a blast of brass as a ragtime tune started up and someone inside the room gave an almost ecstatic sigh.

Time was running out.

I pulled my gun from its holster.

I'd had the silver bullet in its chamber modified, it was hollow, and filled with premium garlic oil. The garlic was totally unnecessary, but I hoped it would cause my quarry additional pain as he died.

I wanted him to feel every agonizing second of it.

I was no sadist but when it came to creatures delighting in long drawn-out deaths, I believed a little karma was apt.

I rushed to the end of the corridor.

The shadow remained fixed on the wall and the swell of trumpets grew louder. I glanced down to see if the charge of magic in my pendant had dimmed. Shit. I reached out; searching for any stray undercurrents of magic I could tap into. There had to be some around with all of Tudor's recent activity.

While I wasn't a magician per se, I was pretty good at finding errant streams of magic. It was like wifi, just waiting to be tapped into as long as I was close enough to the hub. And right now I was about as close to Tudor's magic as I could be. I drew some of his energy in. It swam through me and filled me from head to toe, but its charge was weak.

Tudor had likely exhausted most of its potency when he'd set his traps and masked his true form to seduce his victim. From what I knew of his ways he'd reveal his true face once his prey was about to pass so he could enjoy the bloom of terror through her veins.

I peered around the edge of the door.

The first thing I saw was the blue LED light blinking on the music player sound dock. It rested on an upturned crate next to a sofa that looked like it had been made in the Seventies, and would have been considered bad taste even then.

The woman slumped across it looked old, in her sixties. But then I noticed her clothes and make-up, and realized she was probably in her twenties at best. Her drawn, ashen face was turned towards the ceiling, her mouth slack and eyes wide. She was lost deep inside whatever abyss the drug coursing through her veins had taken her to. It looked like heaven and hell had collided as she grinned and twitched and grimaced.

Tudor sat before her, almost somber in his expensive charcoal grey suit.

He looked like a banker. His dirty blonde hair was slicked back, his pale eyes narrowed with ecstasy. A clear thin tube jutted from his wrist and snaked across the floor to the woman's throat.

The bastard was mainlining her blood.

He reached out with a remote and switched the music to a funereal New Orleans dirge, then he grinned and his eyes flickered like a junkie's. No doubt he was getting high on whatever he'd spiked her with.

My leather bag scraped against the wall as I raised my gun.

The sound jogged him from his trance.

I fired.

Tudor vanished and the bullet exploded into the wall, tearing a hole in the plaster as the oozing IV fell to the floor.

"Morgan Rook." Tudor's words were a warm whisper in my ear. I whirled round and threw a punch that connected with nothing but stale air.

Tudor reappeared on the other side of the room and leaped forward, throwing spells from his sinewy hands. Shadows whirred towards me, magical fear-laced shurikens.

Three of them shot past the side of my face but the fourth found its mark, striking me below the eye with ice-cold precision.

The room vanished and I was thrown back into the past. Back to the asylum. Trapped. Someone shrieked in the darkness, the sound shrill, urgent and primal.

It was a child's cry.

The child was me.

My heart pounded, like it was trying to escape through my ribs. The thought made me want to vomit.

Everything made me want to vomit.

My spirit form shot down a dark corridor, and collided with the boy. I became one with my distant self and looked down to see the hand cradling my own. It was large, calloused and covered in silver scars, but somehow it made me feel warm and reassured.

A loud churning hiss filled the room behind us. The room we'd just left. The room I was even now trying to forget. Goosebumps broke across my ten-year old neck as I turned to look back.

The hall was long and dimly lit, but I could still see the huge canvas hanging on the far wall. It was covered in thick ridges of iridescent black paint that seemed to swirl and shift as I gazed at it. That was the place I'd been born from, one minute nowhere, the next standing in the room with no memories of anything at all. Awake in a new world and doomed to make my way through this dank, broken place.

I tried to look at the man holding my hand, but his face blurred and shifted. He gave my shoulder a reassuring squeeze. "Don't worry," he said. "We're fine now."

A woman cried out somewhere. I leaned over and threw up, and as I straightened, stars exploded before my eyes. The sound of the mounting cries and screams brought me back from the past.

The house on Bury Street reappeared, along with the woman and her pinched, haggard face. Her life, youth and blood was spilling from the IV and pooling across the filthy carpet.

Her eyes found mine and grew bright with panic and realization.

I tried to open my mouth to reassure her, but a fresh wave of nausea stole my words.

"Let's end this nonsense now." Tudor strode towards me, the scalpel in his hand gleaming silver as it plunged towards my heart.

-THREE-

I threw up my arm and Tudor's blade slashed into the wrist guard concealed by the sleeve of my coat. It stuck. I wrenched my arm free and yanked it out.

Tudor began to back away.

I threw the scalpel. It struck him in the center of the chest.

Not one drop of blood spilled from the wound as he pulled the scalpel out and flung it down. The blade tumbled across the floor, chiming like a bell. "You've ruined my shirt," he said. "It's Givenchy." His eyes flitted over my sweater and jeans. "Not that that would mean anything to you."

"My condolences." I reached into my pocket for another bullet and loaded my gun. The weapon was powerful, but it had a serious limitation in that it could only hold a single shot and each cartridge had to be handcrafted.

"Screw you, Rook. You're an affront. A jobsworth for a corrupt outfit."

"I really don't think the boss would describe me as a jobsworth but it's true I enjoy ridding the world of trash like you."

"You're not even one of us. You're blinkered. Humans shouldn't blindly wander into worlds that don't belong to them."

"You might be right, but regardless of what I am," I nodded towards the woman on the sofa. "It's the last time you're going to torture and feed off an innocent. Now, I can make this fast or slow, it's up to you."

Tudor's eyes roved over me, calculating his odds. "How's it up to me?"

"If you tell me something useful, I'll put the bullet in your head, you'll be dead before you know it. Otherwise I'll put it in your stomach and rub salt in the wound."

"What do you mean *useful?"* Tudor took a tentative step towards me.

"I'm looking for Elsbeth Wyght. Do you know where can I find her?"

Tudor grinned. "Oh, I heard about that. She killed your sweetheart, didn't she? And now you're going to make her pay. So noble. So manly. Does the Organization know you're hunting witches on their dime?"

I brought the gun up. "Are you going to tell me where I can find her, or not?"

"I've seen her." Tudor's smiled widened. "We move in some of the same circles. She's a strange one, I'll grant you. Strange and very, very powerful. A true wild child of darkness."

"Where'd you last see her?"

Tudor muttered something.

"What?"

His lips continued to move in a slow, deliberate mumble.

An invocation.

My finger curled around the trigger...and then...

...then he was gone.

A wet, tearing sound filled the room. Tudor reappeared before the haggard girl. A pair of gnarled, leathery wings ripped through the back of his suit and curled up around him, their boney tips clacking together.

All illusion of humanity was gone, in its place, the face of a monster. Gaunt, angular, sunken cheekbones, skin like boiled leather. He looked like something that had spent most of its life in some deep forgotten cave, and for all I knew he had. The black pinpricks in the centers of his pale eyes fizzled and curved teeth jutted from his lips.

His eyes found my throat and I could see his yearning to tear it out and feed, but I also saw his caution as he glanced at the barrel of my gun.

If I missed again, he wouldn't.

"The night is coming." Tudor flexed his long, curled claws.

I fixed my eyes on him, half expecting him to dematerialize. I couldn't miss this time. "It's already night."

"Not this night. *The* night." Tudor gave a smug, contented grin as he swept his withered hand towards the boarded windows. "You've seen the changes. You've felt them. We all have. The city's going to hell and the ones who have kept to the shadows are venturing out. Taking what they want. The horde is at the gates. Can you feel them, Rook? Can you feel their breath on the back of your neck?"

"The only thing I feel is relief, knowing the bullet's spiked with garlic oil. It took a while to get the formula right, but I'm sure a connoisseur like you will appreciate it."

Tudor began to flicker.

I fired.

Into thin air.

The room darkened as he appeared at my side, his teeth sinking into my shoulder. I dropped the gun. It thudded to the floor. The pain in my shoulder was worse than anything I'd ever felt. Like ripping off a bandage and cleaning the wound with sulfuric acid.

I forced myself to stand tall as I waited for my little *surprise* to kick in.

Within moments, he began to howl.

I clapped a hand to the wound on my shoulder. "Essence of hedgeberry. I took a concentrated dose before I got here. It tasted like shit, but it was definitely worth it."

Tudor splayed a hand against the wall as he leaned over and retched. Strings of vomit hung from his mouth as his wings spasmed and thrashed madly. I took his head and slammed it into the wall twice, then dove for the gun.

He fell upon me before I could reach it and scratched at the wound his accomplice had made in my neck. I struggled to right myself while the girl's bare feet twitched on the floor inches from my face.

The room dimmed as Tudor dug further. I couldn't suppress the agony as he grabbed my forehead and his needle-like claws pierced my scalp.

I pulled his finger from the hole in my neck and twisted it until it cracked. Tudor howled and grabbed my head harder, his claws digging deeper. I reached into my bag.

The world turned black. A sharp ringing tone overwhelmed me, and somewhere below it came a faint whimper from the girl on the sofa. It was enough to give me a boost of strength.

My fingers found the pouch I was looking for. I pulled the drawstring loose with my thumb and finger as a wave of searing agony burst through my skull.

Bright, golden light spilled from the bag.

Tudor began to scramble away, his wings jittering, his face a grimace of nausea and disgust. "What's that?"

"This?" I held the pouch up and forced myself to my knees. The room swam around me as I forced a smile. "Sunshine in a bag."

I threw it. His reflexes out-paced his thinking as he opened his hand and the bag landed in his sinewy palm.

He screeched like a child as the glowing light shone upon his face.

I grabbed my revolver and loaded the final bullet into the chamber while he shuffled towards me like a broken automaton.

I fired.

There was a brief flash of light and the bullet smashed into his chest.

Tudor slumped to the floor, his eyes wide and glassy, a vile noxious black stream oozing like ink from the corners of his mouth.

The woman on the sofa stared, but it was clear she wasn't seeing me. Her thoughts were somewhere else altogether. She rubbed her wrists and her hair, as if they crawled with lice.

I rifled through my bag for the pocket where I kept salves and tinctures. Inside was a small silver flask of clear, odorless liquid. A healing water from one of the last truly blessed places. I gently placed the bottle between her cracked lips and tilted it up.

She closed her eyes and swallowed. Slowly her brows un-knitted and a semblance of peace passed across her face. Moments later she slumped over, fast asleep.

. . .

I switched my phone on to find two messages, the first a reminder I'd set months ago.

"Happy Birthday" I mumbled to myself.

In reality there was only a one in three hundred and sixty five chance it actually was my birthday. Because in truth, I had no idea where or when I'd been born, beyond waking up in an abandoned asylum, aged ten.

A couple of years back I'd told this to Willow, the only woman I've ever loved. It was one of the only times I'd ever seen her taken by surprise. She'd given me a long loving look, then drunkenly declared that today would be my birthday. But she was gone now, leaving me to mark the occasion with a girl that looked like a wizened meth head, and the dead vampire at my feet.

The other message was spam from a Gothic dating site that had somehow got my details, which was uncanny given my penchant for wearing black and listening to Nick Cave and The Cure.

I flicked through my address book, which didn't take long, and dialed.

The call was answered mid-ring.

"Dauple," said a wheezy, cracked voice.

"Morgan Rook."

"Morgan Rook!" He repeated, his voice as excitable as a nine year old child on Christmas morning. "You've got something for me?"

“Vampires, two of 'em. Bring bags and a saw. One transformed, so his wings need removing. The only troubling thing about the other one is a seriously bad complexion and a hipster mustache. I'm on Bury Street. How long will it take you to get here?"

Dauple gave a high, manic laugh. "I'm *already* here. Is it safe to come up?"

I shivered. How the hell did he know where I was? "Yeah, it's clear."

The door downstairs slammed, making enough noise to wake the dead. The girl on the sofa stirred. A trace of youth and color had returned to her face but her eyes still had the wild look of a lamb being led to the slaughter.

"You're going to be okay," I kept my voice low and even and it seemed to reassure her. Until Dauple burst into the room, drenched in cheap aftershave that inspired a nightmarish flashback to the eighties.

Dauple looked just as strange and macabre as one might expect from a man that specialized in such a morbid gallows trade. He personified a kid's cartoon sketch of an undertaker, with black shadow-ringed eyes, a long hooked nose and thin curling lips. His drawn face almost glowed white in the gloom as he ran a slow hand through his short thin, coppery hair.

"All dead and broken," he said in a hoarse whisper as he dropped a large metal tool box with a clattering bang.

I did my best not to shudder at the relish in his eyes and the rasp of his long hands as he rubbed them together. "I need you to pack him up and get him and the other one over to the Organization tonight. Okay?"

Dauple nodded, but a distracted gleam lit his eyes. His tongue darted out and slicked his upper lip, then he nodded toward the girl on the sofa. "She's seen better days..." he raised a hand towards her. I slapped it down. "Don't think she's got long," he continued. "Perhaps I should get another bag-"

"Don't touch her." I holstered my gun, then picked up the casings from the floor and slipped them into my pocket. It was doubtful the police would ever visit this squalid place, but I always considered it better to be safe than sorry.

"If you're sure." Dauple sounded disappointed as he began to lay out a long black rubberized body bag. He hummed an off-key tune while he rifled through his case and pulled out a hacksaw.

I watched him and weighed up whether or not I really wanted to engage in further conversation. Then my curiosity got the better of me. "How did you know I was here?"

"I followed you."

"You know where I live?"

Dauple shook his head. "No. Not yet."

"What the hell does that mean?"

"I..." He looked like a child caught stealing a cookie. "I just like to know where the agents live. All the movers, shakers and friends of the crows."

"Why?"

"So I can get to the scene before the retirements happen. "I like to watch things die." He held up a hand and added, "bad things, of course. Not nice things or nice people." Dauple grinned, revealing teeth I didn't want to see.

"Where did you follow me from?"

"The office. I saw you leaving."

He seemed to be telling the truth, but the thought of him tailing me or finding out where I lived made my flesh crawl. "Don't do it again, Dauple. If I find you anywhere near my house, you'll regret it. Do you understand me?"

"Loud and clear."

I looked away as he began to saw through the sinewy joint where Tudor's ragged wings had sprung from his back.

The girl gaped at the spectacle, her face split with horror. I reached into my bag, pulled out a vial of dust, tapped a dose out onto my thumbnail and held it out to her. She took my wrist without a word, put a finger on the side of her nose, pursed her quivering lips, and took a quick short sniff. It was a small dose, just enough to help her forget this night, my face and most of what happened. A little zombification never hurt anyone. At least in moderation.

Dauple began to whistle as he pulled a wing free and laid it down beside Tudor. "I'll need a ride to the hospital when you're done," I told him.

"Rightio!"

I led the girl down the stairs to Dauple's hearse with its fake logo and name for a fictitious undertakers painted on the door. The windows were blacked out and there was no partition between the front and the back so the whole thing reeked of chemicals and things I didn't want to think about. Thankfully the girl didn't notice. I helped her into the back, where she rested on a pile of thick black bags, oblivious to their intended purpose.

I gently closed the door and lay back on the hood of the car while I waited for Dauple to finish up.

The moon hung red and full and its sickly light shone off the windows as a cool breeze stirred the weeds in the gardens. I closed my eyes and did my best to put the evening's events from my mind. I was glad Tudor had been dealt with, but frustrated too because I'd been certain he'd have information on Elsbeth Wyght. He was exactly the kind of creature that evil bitch would associate with. Now anything he might have been able to tell me was taken to the grave, and I was back to square one.

I looked up as Dauple finally exited the house, and got up to help him stow the bodies in the hearse before climbing into the passenger seat.

The drive to the hospital was mercifully quiet, aside from the excitable tap of Dauple's finger on the steering wheel. It was that odd time of year when the last fiery throes of summer were tempered by the imminent arrival of fall. A time of shadows and winds that seemed to hail from somewhere else entirely.

Dauple pulled into the bay outside the emergency room. A tired-looking security guard knocked on his window. I climbed out and gave him *the look.* A *you're wishing you were somewhere else and your gonna forget you ever saw me* look. It took a few seconds to sink in. Most human minds are shockingly easy to manipulate. I suppose it's because we're all so desperate to live in blissful unawareness, especially when it comes to the nightmares that shift and stalk around us. Given the choice, we'll cling to business as usual, whatever the hell that is.

I unlocked the passenger door and helped the girl out. She looked less fatigued now but the black bags under her eyes were still prominent. As were the welts and scratches where she'd attacked the imaginary itch that plagued her wrists.

The hospital receptionist's attractive brown eyes flitted from me to the girl, then back to me with a flicker of disgust. Clearly she thought I was responsible for the girl's state and as I glanced into the large mirror behind her, I saw why.

I looked like shit, my dark clothes ragged and frayed, spatters of blood on my sweater. I pulled my trench coat around me and secured two of the buttons, but it was too late. My throat and face were a map of purple bruises and I looked far older than my thirty something years. I smoothed my dark hair back but the pomade just looked like filthy grease beneath all that overhead lighting.

"What happened to her?" the receptionist asked. The nurse beside her glanced at me, his brow furrowing. He walked towards another security guard and this one seemed more attentive than the one posted outside.

"Someone spiked her drink," I said. I hoped it would stop the conversation, but knew it wouldn't. "You need to get her help."

"I need to get some details-"

I picked up a pen from the clipboard on the top of the desk and reached out for the magic brimming through the hospital. Most of it was weak, but I found enough to charge the pen with a simple spell before passing it to the receptionist. Her pupils dilated, her mouth softened and she gazed up at me, awaiting instructions. "The lady's drink was spiked," I repeated. "She needs urgent attention. You don't need any more details."

The receptionist nodded and called for the nurse. He came over and took the girl's shaking hand. I waited until he led her down the corridor, then I turned on my heels so fast my shoes squeaked on the polished floor. I had to get away from the harsh buzzing lights and the swell of nausea, anguish and pain surging along the corridors.

Dauple was gone by the time I emerged. That suited me. I didn't want the crazy bastard knowing where I was going.

I hailed a cab and slumped in the back. The city passed by in a blur of dark towers and garish lights, and above everything that red swollen moon casting its devilish gleam.

"Happy birthday," I mumbled. There was a bottle of bourbon waiting at the apartment, and sleep wouldn't be too far behind.

Or so I hoped.

-FOUR-

The cab pulled up outside the old Victorian house I called home...well, the top floor at least. The battered old taxi looked distinctly out of place nestled amongst the sleek Audis and BMWs parked along the street.

I paid the driver and waited for him to leave before slipping through the gate and up the flight of wide steps that led to the house. I'd been living here for the best part of a year, but it still amazed me that this was my home. For most of my life my only reason for being anywhere near a nice leafy street like this one was to visit clients. Clients like my landlady, Mrs. Lyra Fitz. I'd met her while moonlighting as Morgan Rook; part-time spiritualist, exorcist and banisher of bad spirits.

Lyra had a particularly nasty problem with a poltergeist in the cellar, and a banshee in the attic. Yeah, she'd really hit the supernatural lottery that year, but it wasn't surprising. Spirits, pucks and spooks were attracted by Lyra's *gift*, as well as that underlying touch of madness she could never quite disguise.

I drove out the unwanted guests and she repaid me by renovating the attic and letting me move in, virtually rent free. Which was a godsend given the cost of living in this city and the paltry wages the Organization paid. It also made me both lodger and caretaker when it came to clearing the premise of any supernatural entities, oddities or occasional insanities.

I slid my key almost soundlessly into the front door and made my way up the flight of plush carpeted stairs as the gentle strains of Erik Satie's 'Nocturne no 1' chimed from Lyra's apartment.

For a moment, I thought I might make it past without her noticing, but a shadow fell across the gap under her door.

The stairs leading to my apartment were so close. If I could just reach...

Click.

The door opened and Lyra appeared. She leaned against the frame, as if posing for a photograph. She looked up at me, elegant even in her bath robe. The shadows accentuated her cut-glass cheekbones and the long silvery blonde hair that was piled high upon her head.

"There you are." Her pince-nez glasses flashed over her azure eyes.

"Here I am." I nodded to the stairs. "I'm just going to-"

"You look terrible, Mr. Rook. And you're hurt!"

I rubbed the bruises on the side of my face. "It's nothing-"

"They're at it again." Lyra stared at me with that singularly unnerving gaze. "The cats." She shook her head. "Plotting."

According to Lyra Fitz the entire planet was controlled by cats. And rather than accept her gift of clairvoyance and second sight, she planted the blame of all visions and odd occurrences squarely upon a feline New World Order. Naturally this was a perfect soup of insanity.

"They must be having a convention," she said.

"A cat convention?"

Lyra narrowed her eyes, as if trying to work out if I was mocking her. I wasn't. I was humoring her.

"The streets were packed full of cats this afternoon. Did you see them? I've never seen so much fur in one day, not since Beijing. They're bringing me nightmares." She shook her head. "Ghastly nightmares."

Her words caught my interest because on top of being a highly gifted empath, Lyra often had prophetic dreams, and more than a few had proved helpful in my investigations. "Nightmares?" I tried to keep my voice as casual as possible.

Her painted eyebrows rose up and she gripped the doorframe with her porcelain-like hand. "I dreamt of a house on a hill, where endless smoke spilled from a canvas. Behind it was a deep black hole."

I did my best to contain the growing unease passing through me and remained silent as I waited for her to continue.

"The black hole pulled everything into it, the earth, the stars, the planets. It smashed them together until they were nothing but dust. And standing behind it all was a man. He waited in the shadows. I could barely see him. His face. It was painted."

"Painted?"

"Yes, white, like a corpse. And he wore a red scarf around his neck, like it was there to hide something. There was sadness, and emptiness in his eyes. And destruction. I didn't like him at all..." Lyra shook her head, and then gave me a weak smile. "Damn cats and their damned nonsense."

I had no idea who the man was, but everything she mentioned harkened back to my hallucination of the asylum. I wanted to press her further, but I could see she was getting agitated and it was late. "Well, you can sleep safe, now, I've locked the door and-"

"They don't need doors. They were in the television earlier, if you please."

I reached out and took her thin hand in mine and gave it a gentle squeeze. "You look tired, Lyra. Get some sleep and try not to worry. I've got everything under control."

She searched my eyes. "If you're sure?"

"Totally sure."

Lyra nodded, stepped back through her door and plunged the hallway into shadows as she closed it softly behind her.

I continued up the stairs to my apartment and opened the psychic locks that sealed the place shut. Usually these kinds of charms only lasted a couple of hours, but there was an almost limitless reservoir of magic surrounding the house. The bulk of it seemed to emanate from the Kabbalist two doors down, the Satanist across the street and the Wiccan in the basement apartment. Tapping into this magic meant I could set a spell that pretty much stayed charged all day.

I looked down as I stepped through the door, eager to make sure none of my guests escape down the stairs. If they did, the jig would be up.

There were only five in the apartment tonight. A Persian on the sofa next to the two Siamese sisters, a Bombay on my turntable, and Alfred, a British Shorthair who liked to sleep on my shoes.

None of the cats were mine, they'd just adopted my apartment as their second home. A place for them to go when they felt like slumming it or having an extra meal.

Their eyes glinted as I lit the candles. "Evening, ladies and gents." Even though I was battered, bruised and totally unnerved, I was glad for their company.

They glanced up with their green, blue and topaz eyes as I made my way through the threadbare apartment and lit the two candles on either side of the framed photograph of Willow. She gazed back, frozen in time, her long brown hair whipped around her in the wind, her hazel eyes mocking me, just as they had when I'd asked her to pose for the picture. I met the ever-wicked smile forever dancing on her lips with my own. The smile I'd never see again.

I kissed my fingers and touched the photograph, then I pulled a bottle of whiskey from the shelf and poured a more than liberal amount into a glass. "If I'm going to get maudlin, I might as well go for the good stuff."

Liquid heat stung my throat as I took a long deep swallow and toasted Willow. "To you, my witchy love. Thanks for the birthday." I emptied the glass and filled it with another generous measure, before heading to the kitchen.

Ten glowing eyes grew wide with anticipation as they scampered to the floor and followed me. I opened a couple of cans of tuna and mashed the contents onto a dinner plate. Even though the brand I bought was nothing like the premium stuff they were probably used to, they still seemed to enjoy it well enough. I set the plate down and they formed a circle of thrashing tails as I slumped onto the sofa.

The television screen stared blankly at me, but there was nothing I wanted to watch. I thought about putting some music on but then the rain began to patter against the roof. I raised my glass toward the ceiling, made a toast and took another long sip.

My phone buzzed with a message; some friends were out in a bar celebrating my birthday for me. I'd planned to be there too but then the intel on Mr. Tudor had come through and diverted me.

As I thought of Tudor, his words came back to me. *The city's going to hell and the ones who have stayed in the shadows are venturing out. Taking what they want. The horde's at the gates.*

Usually I'd take it as nothing more than an empty threat, but then there was Lyra's nightmare and the fact her dreams came to pass way more than I would have liked. No, something was happening out there, something new and malevolent. Something my boss at the

Organization had apparently decided I didn't need to be told about. Being human and on the lowest rung of the company ladder meant I was used to being kept in the dark where intel was concerned. Need to know basis, and all that. But this *was* a need to know situation, for me at least. The whole business reeked of evil, and if there was evil, there was a good chance Elsbeth Wyght wouldn't be far from it.

I considered checking the news for possible developments, but they rarely broadcasted stories that were helpful in my line of work. No, it was all strictly human concerns; murder, rape, corruption, each chasing the other's tail in a vicious circle.

I glanced at my phone, the display reflected my bruised face and the flickering candles behind me as I thought of Haskins. Maybe he'd heard something...

The crossroads beckoned. But instead of four paths, there were two; blissful ignorance, or a Pandora's box. My curiosity outshines caution every single time. Maybe it's why the cats have such a strong affinity with me.

I turned the phone back on and dialed. And then I reached to hang up. There was still time to switch the phone off, to finish the whiskey and lay back and let the world sort itself out.

But that wasn't what I did.

"Haskins."

"It's Morgan."

"What do you want, Rook?"

I took another drink. "Anything happening?"

"Plenty. And..."

"And what?"

Haskins sighed. "And it's late, and I've had a bitch of a day-"

"And what?" I repeated.

"A murder. Weird shit. Must have been done by one of your lot."

By *your lot,* he meant someone into the occult. He wasn't exactly the best at communication, but what he lacked in expression, he more than made up for with stone cold greed. Which meant accessing further information would be easy as long as I was willing to pay. "I can't cross your greasy palms with silver if you won't tell me what happened."

He paused, as if waging a silent battle between his fatigue and greed. "Meet me at the diner. And bring a packet."

A packet meant an envelope with a thousand bucks inside and not a penny less. Covert information sure came at a high price in this city. "I'll be there in half an hour."

"Right." Haskin's siren blared in the background as he hung up.

My arms ached as I pulled on my jacket and glanced at the mirror by the door. My face was pale in the candlelight. I smoothed back my hair and buttoned my collar to cover the bloody wound on my throat. There was nothing I could do about the bruises blooming on the side of my face.

Thankfully the lights were always dim in Nika's Diner.

The cats glanced up as I grabbed my umbrella and a final belt of whiskey.

It was going to be a long night.

-FIVE-

Lunar Avenue was only a couple of turns off the main street that ran through the heart of the city, but almost no one knew about it. A heavy glamour hung over the neighborhood and it worked well in keeping non-magical people out. With me and Haskins, being two of a few exceptions.

I hurried down the sidewalk as the rain thundered down on my umbrella. Nika's Diner was at the end of the road, near a shoe shop that I'd never once seen open in the twenty five years I'd lived here, and a bar called The Lucky Coin.

Sometimes the Coin opened during the day, sometimes at dusk, and if there was any rhyme or reason to its business hours, I couldn't figure it. The place had a reputation for anonymity and easy violence. I'd found more than a few of my charges in there over the years and more than a few of the bloodstains that spattered the sidewalk outside the front door were my own. Which was why I kept my head down tonight, because if I wasn't on Organization business, I wasn't supposed to carry a weapon. Not that I cared but I wanted to stay off the company's radar, for now at least.

My reflection was like a ghost in the diner window. The dingy pink light from the jukebox and faded turquoise formica countertops gave the place a 50s look. Not in a retro way, this place literally hadn't changed for going on seventy years. And it didn't need to, not when it had a captive audience who'd come here no matter what it looked like.

A few customers were huddled in the shadows but the candles on the tables illuminated their faces. Drunks, junkies, dreamers, plotters, planners and people like me engrossed in meetings they probably shouldn't be having.

There was no sign of Haskins.

The door chimed as I shoved it open and stepped inside. The music was perfectly nondescript, easy listening from the 70s. I looked down, trying to avoid eye contact with the people and creatures sitting in the alcoves but I managed to spot a troll who wasn't bothering to cloak himself, as well as a witch and a pair of mages nestled among the usual low life schemers.

The aroma of coffee pancakes and bacon grease hung in the stifling air. I made my way along the counter to the bar stool where Nika, the owner, sat. She was a tall, handsome lady; her thick auburn hair spilled out from under a small white cap and her emerald green eyes glinted like jewels as she glanced up from her magazine.

There was warmth in her eyes, but also tragedy. I'd never asked Nika her story, and she'd never told it, because not asking questions was part of the Diner's allure.

"What can I get you, Morgan?" She asked, her voice as direct and hoarse as ever.

"Coffee." I also ordered a donut I had no intentions of eating. Nika placed it on a china plate, and there it sat, the sugar gleaming on the greasy splodge of dough as she passed me my coffee.

"Keep the change."

She accepted the twenty without a word. Everyone overpaid at Nika's, the diner was both an institution and a haven within the community and we all wanted to keep it that way. I was about to take a sip of coffee when someone appeared in the corner of my eye.

"Detective Haskins." Nika barely kept the disdain from her voice. "Coffee and cheesecake?"

"Yeah, that'll get things started," Haskins answered, just as he always did. He squinted at the bruises on my face and the bloody crust on my neck. "Busy night?"

"Probably about the same as yours." Haskins looked more disheveled than ever. Wild spikes of dirt-brown and ash-grey hair crowned his head. His tired pebble-like eyes were red and his frayed suit seemed like it was about to unravel, I hoped I'd be far away from him when that finally happened.

We walked over to our usual booth at the back of the diner and sat in the shadows beneath the flickering cola sign. Haskins' hands shook as he placed his cup and plate on the table.

He looked haunted. A man with a spectral monkey on his back. He stabbed his fork into his cheesecake and swallowed it without bothering to chew. And then he glanced at me with his usual look of expectation.

I slid the envelope across the table. The irony of having a police detective for a narc wasn't lost on me. "So what have you got?"

Haskins poked at the remains of the cheesecake. "I've spent most of my night at a murder scene. The victim was an older man." He paused and set his fork down. "Someone cut his throat, took his eyes out and laid him on the floor like he was sleeping. He was definitely one of your lot, loads of occult shit in the house."

"Can you elaborate on *occult shit?"*

"Strange old books, black candles, weird statues, hands of glory, that sort of shit." Haskins took the envelope and folded it into his raincoat. "He had some weird scars too."

"Scars?"

"Hocus-pocus symbols. Just above the wrist."

"Scars or tattoos?"

"Both. Rough, like the artist used a knife instead of a tattoo gun."

"What kind of symbols?"

"I don't know what any of that crap means." Haskins shrugged. "I guess they looked like runes."

"They might have been for protection." Protective runes were common in our community.

"Well they weren't very effective, considering...."

"Did you get pictures?"

Haskins pulled out his phone and smeared the display with his greasy thumb as he flicked through it. His face wore a sickly look as he turned the screen my way.

A man, in his late sixties, lay neatly upon polished floorboards with his arms folded diagonally across his chest. A red slash marked his throat and blood pooled around his head like a halo. Flecks stained his white hair and two wet red eye sockets gaped emptily above his drawn lips.

Haskins switched the phone round and thumbed through some more photographs. He pulled one up that showed the faint red rune marked upon the man's wrist.

I felt sick.

I'd seen the symbol before. A friend, of sorts, had the exact same configuration in exactly the same place. I'd only seen it once; the guy wore a raincoat all year round, no matter the season. But I recognized it instantly. It looked like a wheel with nine spiked spokes issuing from its center, the top surrounded by strange, alien writing. "I need a copy of that."

Haskins shook his head. "No. I'm not sending out copies of these pictures. I'm deleting them the minute I leave this place."

I grabbed a pen from my pocket and sketched out the symbol on a napkin, then I asked him for the address of the murder scene. Haskins patted his pocket, no doubt reassuring himself the envelope was still there, and then gave me the location. "You gonna eat that donut?" he asked.

"You can have it."

Haskins wrapped it in a napkin and stood. "Later, Rook."

I nodded. He left the diner, turning the collar of his coat up as he ran for his car. The headlights blazed in the rain as he drove away, passing from the magical quarter back to the city.

The swell of nausea returned as I glanced at the symbol once more.

The victim seemed to be about the same age as my friend, same build too. I took a sip of lukewarm coffee, grabbed my umbrella and headed out, a string of questions churning in my mind.

. . .

The train rattled across the city as crimson moonlight washed over the dark monolithic skyscrapers. An ominous sight, as if some demonic painter had colored the city blood red. It looked unreal, like a backdrop of a movie set.

Haskins' words tumbled through my mind, I kept seeing flashes of the victim and the rune on his wrist. I wondered what it meant, and how my friend Tom had come to have exactly the same one.

I hadn't seen Tom for weeks, but there was nothing unusual there. Like a lot of homeless people, he tended to drift from place to place and then he'd reappear like a forgotten season. But I needed to find him now, make sure he was okay and see if he would tell me what in the hell that symbol meant.

The murder, along with Tudor's warning, pricked me like a rash. Something was happening on my patch, something that Erland Underwood, my boss at the Organization, hadn't bothered to tell me about. I pulled out my phone in case he'd left a message, but there was nothing. Just the one text my girlfriend had sent over a year ago, that I hadn't been able to delete. The last message she'd sent before she'd been murdered.

I thought about calling to demand an explanation but I knew I wouldn't. Underwood and the Organization were my only link to the magical world, and there was no way I'd risk breaking it. At least not until I'd found Elsbeth Wyght and avenged Willow.

The skyscrapers receded, their silhouettes like jagged shards of onyx. The train began to slow.

I got up, jabbed the button until the door opened, and leapt to the platform amid a wash of moonlight that looked like blood.

An ominous sign in what was fast becoming an ominous night.

-SIX-

Cigarette butts, broken bottles and trash littered the street. The sidewalk was pitted, filthy and stained. The shops had security bars on their windows, and the faint glow of televisions flickered in the cramped apartments above.

I checked all the obvious places; park benches, bus stops, dumpsters, doorways, and alleys. I didn't bother with the homeless shelter because Tom seemed to like being on the streets. No, not liked. *Needed* to be on the streets, as if he was constantly protecting his domain.

"Where are you, Tom?" I shone the light from my phone into the gap behind a newsstand, straight into the eyes of an old man huddled under a moth-eaten blanket. I put a couple bucks in his hand and apologized for waking him.

It seemed finding Tom wasn't going to be easy, not that I'd ever actively looked for him before. I'd never actually needed to, thanks to his uncanny knack for turning up, most notably during the more significant events in my life.

Like moments after the first, and last, beating I received on my third day of high school. Or when he'd arrived just as my foster father kicked me out onto the street, his evil twisted girlfriend hanging off his arm. My father had stuffed my clothes and what little I owned into a trash bag and mumbled something about being sorry, and how it was for the best. Well, it was for him at least.

But as I'd seen his disgusting girlfriend's grin, I'd lost it. Thankfully Tom had appeared at that moment and pulled me away, but not before making me take back the flippant curse I'd thrown at the bitch.

Words have power.

I still remember Tom saying that, and the look in his eyes. I'd apologized and backtracked immediately, because somehow Tom, a ragged homeless man, carried more authority than any cop or judge I'd ever encountered.

The last time I'd seen him was just after Willow's murder. He'd been standing on a street corner feeding breadcrumbs to a pigeon. He'd offered me a drink from a bottle of grim booze that was tucked inside a crumpled paper bag. Then we found a bench, sat and stared off, each in our own world until Tom spilled booze on his raincoat and I'd watched as he stood to take it off, for what seemed the first time ever.

That was when I'd noticed the symbol on his arm. I asked about it and he'd said something I hadn't understood. Then I'd just sort of forgotten about it. As if the question had never crossed my mind in the first place.

A smash and a tinkle of glass brought me back to the present. The scrap of land below the overpass had become a growing camp for the homeless. A place for the specters the city had tried to hide, to meet and trade information or insults, to scrap and confer. Fires blazed in old rusted metal barrels, and painfully thin people gathered around for warmth.

Someone stumbled along the sidewalk, their eyes wide below wild wiry hair. It took me a moment to realize it was a woman and for the moonlight to reveal the large purple bruise below her eye. She gave me a skittish, panicked glance and edged towards the street.

"I'm looking for someone.You might know him, his name's Tom and-"

She pointed towards the end of the street. "He's in the alley with the bad men." Her hand strayed to the bruise below her eye. "Really bad men."

"Did they do this to you?"

She nodded. "They said they were going to set fire to me but Tom came...he told me to go. So I did."

My shoes pounded the road as I ran, the moonlit world jolting around me, all hard black edges and red and silver shadows. Nausea flooded through me as I thought of the victim from Haskins' photograph.

Throat slashed, eyes removed.

I ran past figures huddled against the wall in sleeping bags, my shoes crunching slivers of broken glass. Braying laughter echoed from the alley as I turned the corner, followed by a savage, excited shout.

Five men surrounded a doorway. I could just make out Tom behind them, his back to the door, facing them head on. His long grey white hair was swept back in a pony tail, and he had one hand out before him, as if to push them away, the other inside his battered old raincoat.

I pulled a shard of quartz crystal from my pocket and let the magic flow through me. The charge swept from my hands to the center of my skull. It felt like tiny fireworks were igniting in my mind. I reached out and tapped the air for more power, but there was scant magic in this forlorn place.

Tom glanced at me as I approached the group and shook his head, then the thugs turned my way.

They were garden variety pricks, fresh from a late night bar and an evening of rejections from women wise enough to see the savagery below their smart clothes and expensive aftershave.

"What the fuck are you looking at?" The closest asked. He was short and ripped, but I could still see the weak, fat little kid he'd once been. I scanned the rest of the group. They were a good ten years younger than me, and by the way they positioned themselves, used to fighting in a pack.

The only one that worried me was the one near the dumpsters. There was a snide, low cunning look in his eyes as he stooped down, spilled a bag of clothes and tore off a strip of fabric.

And then I saw the bottle of Everclear at his feet and I knew with sickening inevitably what was about to follow.

-SEVEN-

The rest of the pack of drunken thugs looked from Tom to me, uncertain where to strike first. I used their moment of indecision to my advantage and leapt into the fray. Mr. 'What the fuck are you looking at?' pulled back his fist. I jammed the heel of my hand into his solar plexus and as he buckled over, drove my knee into his face.

Two more ran at me. I sidestepped them and grabbed the closest and threw him into the other. They went down in a tangle of limbs and slurred curses.

My attention turned to the one lighting the molotov cocktail. It flared up with a burst of blue and orange light that cast a hellish glow across his face. His eyes danced with a hunger for suffering, and easy casual violence.

Time seemed to slow as he pulled back the bottle.

"Tom!" I yelled.

Tom was busy fighting off the other assailant, but he managed to turn away from the full impact of the bottle as it shattered on the door behind him and sent spatters of molten fire across his coat.

The thrower's eyes grew wide as he watched, hypnotized by the flames.

I was on him in a stride and punched him hard in the face.

His expression contorted to agony, and then fury. I grabbed his head with both hands and stared into his eyes. "Look at me," I growled. "Look at me."

Rage, hatred and spite flitted through his hateful, devious gaze. And then his eyes grew wider as he saw my *other side*. The dark, shadow-self I've spent the best part of my life running from.

He tried to squirm away but I held him firm.

"You see it," I said. "Don't you?"

He whined as I pulled him closer, the magic flowing through me revealing flashes from his life. Of the kid he'd led into the woods when he was a child himself, and the relentless beating that had followed. Of the sick pulse of adrenaline that had surged through him as he'd thrashed the boy within an inch of his life. He'd gotten away with it, and that victory had only served to encourage the spree of cowardly bullying violence that had followed.

I saw it all.

The people he'd preyed on for money, the arson and cruel petty vandalism.

The rape of the teenage neighbor he was contemplating.

The bottomless pit of sadism and hatred in his soul.

But it paled to nothing as he looked into my eyes. He began to spasm and shake.

"Do you want it to stop?" I asked.

Tears sprung in his eyes. He nodded.

"Then end it all tonight," I said. "Kill yourself. Do you understand?"

He nodded again.

I turned as footsteps pounded behind me. A ringed fist thudded into the side of my face. Black stars jittered across my eyes and a low, flat whine filled my ears. I let go of the arsonist and spun round as one of the other thugs bore down on me. I watched as he pulled his fist back, I grabbed it and twisted his hand until something snapped in his wrist.

His howl broke as I kneed him hard in the balls and watched him drop to the ground.

Fighting drunks felt like having superhuman powers. It was almost too easy.

Tom had the last one in a stranglehold. He squeezed until the man's eyes glazed over and he lost consciousness, then Tom glanced up at me. "You shouldn't have done that."

"There's gratitude," I said.

"I meant the hex." He gave me a stark, accusing look.

I glanced at the sadistic thug. He was shaking uncontrollably as he stared at the ground. "The world's better off without him-"

"It's not for you to judge," Tom said. "Or to pass sentence. Believe me, that kind of condemnation can destroy your life." His eyes blazed at me. "Undo it."

As much as it pained me, I knew he was right. I removed the hex, but left a nasty little something behind. A failsafe, a nightmare beyond any nightmares that pig had ever known. It would appear the very moment he attempted to harm anyone and it wouldn't relent until he was reduced to a gibbering wreck fit for the nuthouse.

I joined Tom as he stepped over the sprawl of groaning bodies. He reached to pull a flask from his pocket and his coat sleeve rode up, revealing the bottom of the symbol. It looked old, but the scar was still livid red. I pointed to it. "What does it mean?"

Tom took a swig from his flask, swallowed, and shook his head. "Nothing to you. I appreciate your help, Morgan, but I could have dealt with them on my own. It happens all the time."

As we walked, the lights from the street covered the alley's entrance in a sodium glow. Tom's eyes were clouded, haunted.

Something had its claws in his back and it wasn't just the booze.

"What are you doing here, Morgan?"

"Looking for you. A man was killed tonight, he had the same tattoo." I saw the glimmer in his eye. He already knew. "What's it all about?"

"It's just a mark between friends."

"It's more than that. I need to know, it's my job-"

"And how is the Organization these days? They treating you well?" There was irritation in his voice but then his scowl softened. He took another drink and passed the flask to me. I savored the soft spread of numbness as it countered the fire that still raged through my frayed nerves.

"Tom?" I asked.

He took the flask back and slipped it into his coat. "I lost a good friend tonight and now I'm going to drink enough to forget the world. Go, Morgan. Get out of the city, stay away for as long as you can. Or better still, don't come back."

"I can't leave. It's home."

"Is it?" There was a strange edge to his voice.

"I'm concerned about you." I was determined to take back control of the conversation. To show him I was no longer the little kid with the scraped knees and the chaotic life. "I need to know what it means."

"Like I said, it's a symbol of fellowship. And it's private."

I could see he wasn't going to be drawn any further. "Fine. I'll stop asking. Please tell me you've got somewhere safe to sleep until this blows over."

"Sleep's the last thing I need." His laugh was short and bitter. "Sleep gets you killed." He led me to the end of the alley. "I can look after myself, Morgan, but life will be a lot easier if I don't have you to worry about. Think about what I said. You've seen the changes and it's going to get a lot worse. Dark times are coming, and with them an evil I thought I'd left in a place so far from here. But then we never actually escape our past, do we? Not really."

"Quit the cryptic mumbo-jumbo, Tom. I'm trying to help you."

Tom's nostrils flared as he took a deep breath. "You can almost smell the darkness it's so close...."

All I could smell was stale urine, exhaust fumes and rotting garbage wafting from the alley. Tom stopped as a police car drove past and the cop inside glanced our way. I matched her gaze as if I had nothing to hide and absolutely nothing to do with the groaning men sprawled out in the alley behind us. She drove on.

"Go, Morgan. We'll talk later, when it all blows over."

There was a horrible finality in his voice and a steeliness in his eyes that wouldn't break. He glanced to the alley across the street. It was dark, almost impossibly black, but I could make out the hood of a silver sports car, long like a Jaguar. The engine hummed but the lights remained off as it rolled back into the gloom.

I was about to start towards it, when Tom gripped my arm. "Let go of the past, Morgan. Make a new future. You've a foot in two worlds. Ground yourself in the here and now. Live, enjoy life. Whoever said ignorance was bliss was right. Now, promise me you'll leave."

I didn't tend to back down much, but I found it impossible to match the hard glint in his eye. So I nodded, and lied. "Sure, I'll take a vacation."

Tom smiled and clenched my shoulder before walking back into the shadows. I watched until he was gone, then I made my way through the knot of back streets until I reached civilization.

I flagged down a cab, sat in the backseat and gazed out at the drunks and clubbers as they shuffled through the streets like zombies. The moon above them shone bright and hard, turning the city to red and black.

-EIGHT-

A dull, familiar whine woke me as Mrs. Fitz blended something in her kitchen. It felt like I'd had an hour's sleep at best, but the clock told me I'd had just over three. I sat up on the sofa and gazed at the whiskey glass on the armrest beside me. Its partner in crime, the empty bottle on the table, seemed to glint almost accusingly in the early morning light.

Not the smartest way to get to sleep, but it masked the aches and pains for a few hours. Until I made the mistake of standing and they returned in full righteous vengeance.

The events of the previous night swam through my mind along with all the questions that needed answering. I picked up the phone and rang Underwood. It went straight to voicemail.

"It's Morgan." My voice was cracked and hoarse. "We need to talk." My scrambled brain ran out of words so I hung up and decided to go see him, rather than wait for a reply that probably wasn't coming.

I stooped down and gathered up the cats that had curled up on the sofa around me in the wee hours, carried them to the dormer window and gently deposited them on the roof below. They arched their backs and slunk off toward the street in search of breakfast.

It was a balmy day but the breeze held a chill. Autumn was coming, and hard on its heels another long winter. The dark months were always my busiest time and with the way things were going with the Nightkind, it was shaping up to be a hard season.

A dangerous one too. Which meant the sooner I found the murderer, and put them out of action, the better. That way Tom would be safe and I could give my full attention to my pet project, Elsbeth Wyght, before things started to really heat up.

I glanced at the photograph of Willow. "I'll get the bitch. I swear it."

I showered and made toast, grabbing a couple of bites as I hurried down the stairs, doing my damnedest not to chew as I crept past Mrs. Fitz's apartment.

The last thing I needed right now was any more talk of global feline conspiracies.

Especially when I'd just rushed out the door with my sweater and coat covered in multiple shades of fur.

...

The Organization's offices were downtown above a Chinese market, and there was a blink and you'll miss it doorway right beside their service entrance. As in most cities, the majority of the shoppers and pedestrians just hurried past, but there was an enchantment that cloaked the building just in case we got any snoops or looky-loos. It was a clever little spell because anyone considering intruding here would find the thought snatched right out of their heads. It was funny to occasionally see people's knitted brows, their faces turned heavenwards as they tried to work out the really important thing they'd just forgotten.

The small brass plaque beside the door reads, "Messrs. Humble, Glass and Underwood Investigative Services" and the font made it look like it was created in the nineteen twenties. Hell, it probably was.

I pushed the door open and the smell of the market wafted over the narrow flight of steps, aniseed, dried fish and durian. Cigar ash spotted the worn maroon carpet and a fresh fall indicated Underwood was already inside.

The frosted glass door at the top of the stairs was branded with the company's logo, a triangle with an eye at each point and a flaming eye in the center. An additional deterrent for any uninvited guests who might make it past the enchantment downstairs. Eyes and triangles already had a tendency to unsettle people but this emblem was a warning that was even more primal. Ignore those gut feelings and the hex on the threshold would produce a debilitating migraine that'd bring an unauthorized intruder to their knees. It was apt, as I often found dealing with the the Organization to be one long headache.

I shoved the door and stepped into the sparse office. The place was almost padded with silence. No phones, no secretaries tapping and clacking on keyboards, no 'witty' signs proclaiming *you don't have to be mad to work here but it helps*. No monochrome pictures of beaches and inspirational quotes. Just a waiting room and three offices enclosed with partitions of dark paneled wood and frosty pebbled glass, one for each of the partners.

The waiting room was a dismal square of grey with a worn leather sofa and two chairs, all of them occupied. I recognized three of the agents. Two were colleagues, one a bounty hunter. But the fourth...I didn't know anything about the fourth, and instincts told me I didn't want to get anywhere near him.

Raspink sat in the closest seat, towering over the others. His long lean face was pale and lined, his gaze thankfully lost in the woven pattern of the threadbare carpet. I'd give almost anything not to have to meet that cold dead stare.

Beside him sat Ebomee, a black woman in her mid twenties. Today she wore an elegant slate-grey suit and the smile she gave me didn't quite reach her quick, searching eyes. I smiled back. It always seems the best policy to promptly return any courtesies when dealing with highly trained assassins.

Two men sat on the sofa. The nearest, Osbert, looked like an obese teenager with floppy red hair and wide, gimlet eyes. His mouth was a thin line defined solely by the brass ring piercing his top lip. Beneath this *man suit*, Osbert was an ogre and he had a particular fondness for ripping out the hearts of his foes. He glanced at me and grunted before delving back into his bag of chips.

The three of them were troubling enough, but none could hold a candle to the man on the end of the sofa.

He wore a long coat and his wide-brimmed hat threw restless shadows that seemed to crawl across his face. Shadows that, given the early morning light, were nothing less than unnatural. He began to turn towards me. I glanced away toward Underwood's door.

Underwood was a black and lilac blur behind the frosted glass. Someone sat opposite him and their were voices muffled. His office was situated in-between the offices of the other two partners, Humble and Glass. I'd worked for the Organization for seventeen years and I'd never seen either of them. And I was fine with that.

A monotonous fluorescent buzz fell over the waiting room broken only by the sound of Osbert's fingers as he dug for the last crumbs of his greasy golden breakfast.

Finally, Underwood's voice began to rise and whoever was in there with him stood and opened the door. A short dumpy woman with a red face and thick glasses emerged. She glared at me as she slammed Underwood's door, and thundered from the offices.

"Rook." Underwood's soft, sardonic voice issued from his room.

I stepped into his small plush office and closed the door, glad to put something between myself and the freak show seated outside. Underwood sat behind his desk, the glare from the window behind him spreading like a halo around his head.

If I had to guess, I'd say he was in his late fifties, give or take a couple of centuries. Long strawberry blonde hair framed his face and his fae, lilac eyes matched the tie resting neatly against his crisp white shirt. The golden ring in his ear gleamed as he glanced up at me, steepled his fingers and gave me a crooked smile. "I don't remember setting up an appointment. So imagine my surprise at seeing your black-clad form through the glass." His keen eyes ran over the bruises on the side of my face. "I see Mr. Tudor put up a fight."

"He did. Along with the other vampire."

Underwood nodded. "Apologies for that. I only had intelligence for Tudor. Still, Dauple assured me you dispatched both of them quite adequately. By now they'll be no more than vampiric cinders floating over the city. Well done, Rook. Tea? Coffee?"

"No thanks."

Underwood's rested his long chin on his steepled fingers. "I don't have any work for you, if that's what you've come for."

"I'm surprised to hear that. It seems the whole city's going to hell right now."

"Things are certainly...ramping up, shall we say." Underwood lifted a china cup from its saucer and took a sip, the gesture as genteel as everything else about him.

"I know about the murder."

"Which one?" Underwood asked, but I could see he knew exactly what I was talking about.

"The occultist that had his throat cut, his eyes removed and his arms folded over his chest like he was sleeping. My contact told me the forensics team has nothing to go on."

"We're looking into it."

"We?"

His eyes narrowed. "Mrs. Glass and myself. But I fail to see why this is of any interest to you."

"The murder happened on my patch and the victim had runic markings identical to a friend of mine's tattoos. I'm worried there might be a connection."

Curiosity flashed in Underwood's eyes. "And who might this friend be?"

"No one. What can you tell me about the killer?"

Underwood's eyes grew hard and his irises darkened to obsidian. " My colleague's working this case. Her and her assets. Ergo you're not."

"Why didn't you think it was worth mentioning to me?"

The side of Underwood's face reddened. "You seem to have a shaky grasp of which of us is the employer, and which the employee. I tell you what you need to know. And right now, I'm telling you to back off."

"I can't." My knuckles grew white as I gripped the edge of the desk. "Not if my friend's in danger. I need to find the killer."

Underwood's tone dropped to a low, dangerous growl. "It's being dealt with and isn't open for discussion. Stay out of it, Morgan. Agents that disobey often find themselves touring Stardim."

I suppressed a shiver as thoughts of Stardim filled my mind; its high security walls, guard towers and the violent supernatural criminals festering within its cells. Almost no one that went in ever came back out, and those that did rarely reoffended.

Underwood's gaze was hard and I was forced to look away from the raging fire dancing behind his eyes. And then he smiled, reached into his desk and pulled out an envelope. "You did a good job with Tudor and his acolyte. It would have been better if you'd taken them alive, but dead has its benefits too."

He slid the money towards me, leaned back and for a moment it looked like he had something else to say. Then he shook his head and gestured to the door. "Go, Morgan. Take a break."

It was the second time I'd been told that in less than twenty four hours.

I nodded, left the room and did my best not to look back at the figures in the waiting room as I headed for the door.

A nod wasn't a lie.

-NINE-

Since I was about to do exactly what Underwood told me not to do, I figured why stop there?

I walked a couple of blocks south of the Organization's offices and stopped outside a video rental shop called Electric Video Club. The place looked as dead as ever and rarely had customers, asides from the odd nerd looking to add to his Betamax collection, or treasure hunters searching for rare and valuable horror on VHS.

Which was exactly its point.

I stood before the shop's shuttered window and glanced through past the dust-laden video cassettes, their once garish covers washed out and bleached by time. Thick murky darkness gathered beyond the display.

The door needed an extra shove, which was another slight but deliberate deterrent. I stepped inside. Madhav sat behind the counter staring at his phone. He glanced up and gave a slight nod as I walked past. "Morning," I said.

"Indeed."

I liked Madhav, he was a man of few words. I made my way down a long aisle of videos, the faces staring out from the covers snapshots from a bygone era.

At the back of the aisle was a heavy metal door and an illusion. A sort of trompe l'oeil that hung in mid air and gave a very real impression of a storeroom filled with boxes, broken video players, and a rusty stepladder.

I walked through them and entered the large room beyond.

The Armory.

Weapons covered the walls: assault rifles, sniper rifles, handguns of every make and model. Below them were rows of squat glowing glass cabinets filled with crystals that threw deep washes of color out into the room. Purple that sparkled from charged amethyst was tempered by the otherworldly glow of moonstones. The rest of the rainbow burst forth from calcites, fluorites, quartz and crystals I had no name for.

The whole room hummed with magic.

"Morgan Rook," A rumbling voice boomed from the backroom. Bastion Stout appeared, his head barely cresting the top of the counter. For some reason he was wearing a classy black suit today that made him look like a diminutive but powerful bouncer. His fierce eyes brooded up at me from below his heavy brow. He pulled himself up onto the stool and gave me the amused look he always seems to have when we need to talk shop. Then he stroked his beard. "What do you need, refills?"

"Yeah. I'll need some new crystals. Ammo too, and a couple of handguns couldn't hurt." I tried to sound as casual as possible.

"Right you are. How many crystals?"

"Ten or so. And pendants if you have any to spare."

Bastion's eyes swept over me. "Where's my empty crystals?"

"At home. Sorry."

"And the release form for the new equipment?"

"Also at home."

Thankfully Bastion was used to this, and even though he'd warned me countless times about not returning equipment after a job, he always let it slide.

"I have a list you know," Bastion said as he slid open the weapons cabinets and packed a canvas satchel. He pointed to various guns and waited for me to nod or shake my head. "Every single piece of Organization equipment you've failed to return has been itemized. I keep it hidden from Snarksmuth you'll be glad to know."

Snarksmuth's the other armorer, a jobsworth and all-round pain in the ass.

"So what's your assignment?" Bastion asked as he picked through a tray of amulets.

"It's strictly hush hush." I took no pleasure in lying, but with Underwood demanding I take time off, I needed to grab what I could, while I could.

"Fair enough." Bastion opened up the padded section at the top of the satchel and placed a handful of crystals inside. "The armory's been doing a brisk trade these last few days."

"Have any other agents been in?"

"Oh yes.' He scowled. "Loathsome, creepy bastards. Bitches too. You're one of the few I can deal with." He shook his head. "Sometimes I wonder what Messrs. Humble, Glass and Underwood are thinking."

"Me too."

'But I suppose dark times need dark measures," Bastion growled. "Things seem to be getting worse by the day. I've lived here for decades, you know and there's always been ups and downs, but lately..." He climbed up onto the stool and placed the satchel on the counter. "Lately I've thought about packing up and leaving."

"The city?"

"*The world*. My homeland's no picnic, what with the endless wars. But this place seems to be getting completely out of hand. I swear it's only a matter of time before the blinkered wake up to us, and..." Bastion held a hand up. "I'm sorry Morgan. No offense intended."

"None taken. I'd join you in world trotting if I could. It'd be nice to be somewhere else for a while. Sample new beers and maybe even some culture. And then more beers."

Bastion laughed. "Believe you me I could take you on many an Inn crawl. Maybe I will, if we can find a way to move a human between worlds."

"Count me in." I picked up the satchel. "Seriously, I hope you're not going to leave. But if you do, let me know ahead of time so I can give you a proper send off, complete with the mother of all hangovers. Right?"

"Right." Bastion's grin turned to a scowl as the door in the small room behind him clanged. He glanced at his watch. "Snarksmuth's early. You better go. Just make sure you bring me the forms for that stuff. Right?"

"I will. Take care."

I hated lying to Bastion, but needs must when the devil drives.

-TEN-

I returned to my apartment to rethink my situation. Clearly Underwood wasn't talking, and as for Tom, I'd be better off trying to wring blood from a rock. I called Haskins but he had nothing new.

It wasn't the first dead end I'd ever reached in an investigation. I just needed to look a little harder, find some new stones to kick over.

The coffee cup warmed my hands as I sat back on the sofa and closed my eyes. I could sense magic thrumming in the air just outside the window. Someone was conducting a ritual, it was a great connection but I had no need to tap in. The thing is, using it comes at a cost and after all these years, I've never found a way around that. Magic supercharges the senses and gives all sorts of gifts, but go too far with it and the comedown is horrendous and makes the aftermath of a two-day drinking binge seem like a picnic.

I glanced at the table and the napkin with the victim's address. I typed it into my phone and looked it up on a map. It was only a few blocks away.

I glanced out the window as the sun emerged from the clouds and illuminated the distant skyscrapers. B&E at a crime scene was definitely a covert operation so I decided to grab a few winks while I waited for the cover of night.

I ditched the coffee, grabbed a fresh bottle of whiskey and took a good hard swig. It numbed my senses and slowed my racing mind. I sank into bed, kicked off my shoes and fell into a deep, but fitful sleep.

. . .

My phone chimed at half past six, waking me from a torrent of strange, unsettling dreams. I tried to recount them as I untangled myself from the blankets but my tentative grasp on the details had evaporated.

I drew back the blinds. The sun had slipped behind the hills, the city lights twinkled in the dusk and a breeze with a distinct autumnal chill whistled through the gap in the window.

The coffee maker gurgled as I placed my leather bag on the table and restocked it with items from the supply satchel. First, I grabbed half a dozen charged crystals, a spare gun, and a silver bladed knife. Then I checked my med kit, replenished the cures and salves, and packed an Organization-issued compass that tracked supernatural entities. Finally I secured a moonstone pendant around my neck and shivered as the magic inside tingled against my skin.

My laptop flickered as I flipped up the screen and waited for the hard drive to sputter to life. There was no news worth noting. A bank robbery, a couple of hold-ups, a suicide on the subway, and a shoot-out between rival gangs. The usual.

The bathroom filled with steam as I ran a shower and let the hot water pound and scorch my skin. It's good to purify and focus before going out on a job. It keeps the mind sharp.

I climbed out of the shower, cleared a space on the mirror, shaved and dressed. Black jeans, black sweater, black shoes. Which seemed oddly appropriate for visiting a murder scene. I returned to the living room to find it filled with cats. I opened some tuna for them and slipped out into the night.

. . .

The crime scene was on the top floor of a large broad apartment building with a fire escape that ran up one side. Perfect.

I didn't head there straight off. Instead I climbed to the roof of the building next door. A variety of scents wafted along in the cool breeze. It seemed like every savory dish in the world was being cooked below me and the air was filled with garlic, spices and onions. I pulled a telescope from my bag and swept it over the neighborhood.

The murder was already old news so the place was free of cops, and I didn't see any signs of The Organization either. Two prostitutes swapped tattle and dirty laughs on the corner and a gang of wannabe hoodlums on BMXs loitered across the street.

The cars parked along the road were empty, except one. Steam fogged the windshield blurring the silhouette inside.

I put on my Organization shades and scanned the car. A single red and purple heart raced behind the glass and steel.

Excited.

I focused harder, trying to get more of a sense of the person or creature inside. No, it was a man, his heart coursing with nerves and adrenaline.

Was he watching the apartments?

No, his eyes were fixed on the hookers, his mind rife with indecision. A nervous customer window-shopping. No threat to me or them.

I double checked the other houses and apartment buildings, but the place looked clear. I made my way down the stairs and slipped through the narrow walkway between the two buildings.

The ladder on the fire escape above me was out of reach. I rolled a dumpster beneath it, jumped and pulled myself up to the bottom rung.

I climbed cold squeaking metal steps to the top and edged along the landing to the apartment. The window was locked. I grabbed a crystal, drained it of power and imagined the latch sliding open.

Click.

I slid the window open and waited to make sure the darkened room was empty. It seemed to be, but appearances could be deceiving so I slipped the shades back on and did a quick scan, scouring the apartment for heartbeats other than mine.

There was nothing except for a couple of rats in the walls.

I climbed inside and set my foot down on the shag carpet.

The place smelled of blood and death, cheap cologne and frustration. Cops and forensics had been over every inch of the place, before finally giving up. They'd found nothing. But I didn't needed magic to tell me that, when a simple call to Haskins had sufficed.

It was a small pokey place and it seemed like the man who'd lived here had done so for a very long time. Everything was dated and the furniture didn't look like it had been moved for decades.

The room was like a study or a home office but there was a total lack of technology.

No computer, phone or tablets. No television, radio or DVD player. Nothing modern. Plenty of occult paraphernalia and dust. Plus books. Lots and lots of books.

I ran my flashlight over the spines of encyclopedias, dictionaries, travel guides, and how-to books for simple, basic things. Stuff most people would have learned before they'd finished high school. I wondered if the victim might have immigrated here but there was nothing that indicated this, no particularly ethnic objects, foreign art or souvenirs.

The adjoining bookcase was more like what I'd expected, thick dusty books primarily focused on magic, mythology and ritual. This wasn't as rare as it might have been before. People's interest in magic was growing. When I'd started at eighteen, I'd felt like I'd been in a tiny, exclusive club. But not anymore. Now it seemed like every man, woman, child, and their dog, was into magic.

Maybe it was the proliferation of science and technology that made it seem like more of the world's esoteric mysteries should have been solved by now, but there were plenty that hadn't been. And while humanity might have better lenses to see the universe through, they often missed what was right before their eyes as they overlooked beings that, via a small shift in perception, choose not to be seen.

"Interesting." There was a discrepancy between these books and the ones on the prior shelf. Thee others had covered topics like basic cooking, English and general knowledge but these magical books were advanced, delving into subjects like defenses against demons, invocations, and necromancy theory as well as practice.

I pulled my phone from my pocket and photographed the titles, in case I needed to refer back to them later, then I stepped into the center of the room. It was time to do a little traveling.

The crystals crackled as I pulled them from my bag and clutched them in my hands. I shivered as the electric-like charges ran through the palms of my hands and spread through my body. I began to intone one of the last spells my trainer at the Organization had shown me.

In a way it was like time travel, but really it involved projecting the spirit form back into the past. Just like Tudor's trap had done, only this time I was in control.

The magic continued to pulse from the crystals, running through my veins like liquid fire. I shuddered and closed my eyes to focus and harness its power.

Silence fell over the world and all I could hear was the beat of my heart, and the thump of blood in my ears. I ignored it all and allowed myself to stray from my suit of flesh and bone, to drift out into the room around me.

I turned and saw myself standing there, eyes closed, hands open, the crystals glowing in my palms. Time swept around me with a roar and a crash, as a sea of gaseous swirling colors enveloped me. I waited until I found a twisting grey stream that ran back into the past.

I stepped into it and watched like a ghost as the apartment fell empty. Night became day, and then night once more. Then the lights came on in the very same room where my future unobservable self waited along a finite filament of time. Cops and forensics went about the painstaking business of scouring for evidence and I was like a fly on the wall.

The scene passed in time-lapse, and soon the torches and lamps faded and night filled the empty room with murk and shadows.

I stepped into the stream again and went further back, until finally I arrived at the night of the murder.

There was a presence now, two people. One in the hallway, the tenant, or soon to be victim, and the other...I could feel their essence, and yet a part of it remained elusive.

A blur of movement came from the window, a dark hooded figure on the fire escape. Its silhouette was slender and I couldn't tell if there was a man or woman below its long black cloak.

I sailed across the room, passed through the glass and merged with the mysterious figure.

It was like stepping from a steaming hot shower into an icy storm.

Shock and panic jittered through my spirit form, it took everything I had not to slip away, to be thrust back toward the future, back to the time and place where my body stood, entranced.

Who or whatever they were, they were as cold as the grave. I could hear no sense of self inside them, no heartbeat, no emotions.

Just intent.

An intent to murder.

They glanced down at the window and the magical spell sealing it shut. The locks had been bewitched so even the slightest move to unbind them would alert the tenant.

I could read the assassin's thoughts, limited though they were in sense its calculations. Its prey was armed and powerful, it had magic. Old magic. While the killer had no powers, it was ruled by the sorcery that commanded it, allowed it to move and think in its limited terms.

The assassin stood at the window, as if waiting for something. What?

A distant voice flashed inside its mind, a whisper. The sound sent a jolt of icy cold horror through my soul. It was a man's voice, soft, well spoken, powerful. And familiar?

Whispering instructions directly into the killer's mind.

The assassin intoned the words, mirroring the voice as it ran a hand over the window disarming the spells. Then it watched as the magical traps faded and winked out.

The locks flicked open, just as they had for me, only this time they were virtually silent. The puppeteer that controlled this deadly automaton wielded magic far more powerful and accomplished than mine.

I was little more than a helpless observer as the assassin slid the window open and climbed inside, its footfall silent, its mind primed to kill.

-ELEVEN-

The assassin crossed the room and the hanging light fixture illuminated its form as it stepped into the hallway. It passed a mirror, revealing the wooden mask that covered its face, and the dull gleam of its cloudy blue eyes. Dead, corpse-blue eyes.

A sheathed sword hung by its side, held in place by a thick black belt laden with leather pouches. Its footfalls were almost silent as it stalked toward the light and sounds that emanated from the room at the end of the hall. A scrape of cutlery on china, running water, a television blaring a documentary.

The assassin dug into one of its pouches and produced a blowgun and a single glass-tipped dart. It was hollow and something moved within the glass, like a stringy form of living moss. Tiny green tendrils unfurled as the assassin held it up to the light.

A chair scraped across the floor in the room as it approached, followed by a wet, phlegmy cough. The assassin reached for the doorframe and peered inside.

A tall, heavy man stood by the kitchen sink. His salt and pepper hair was cropped short, and silvery hairs sprung from the neckline of his t-shirt and ran to the nape of his reddened neck. He scrubbed a plate with a sponge, his attention on the television that sat above the fridge.

The assassin raised its blowgun.

"Get down!" My words were silent, I had no voice.

The assassin blew.

I watched as the dart glinted through the air.

It struck the back of the man's neck. He swore, and batted at the wound, leaving soap suds on his t-shirt. Then he gave a choked cry as he collapsed against the sink.

His face was a brutal, livid purple, his eyes filled with shock. They grew wider as his gaze fell upon the assassin. "Damn you!" he growled as he pulled a carving knife from a drawer, sliced at the air and staggered across the kitchen.

The assassin stood and watched impassively.

"Who sent you..." The man began to cut at the back of his neck, desperately trying to prize the dart free. His fingers came away red with blood. "Who?"

"Sleep." The assassin answered, its voice hoarse and dry.

The man stumbled as if he were standing upon the deck of a surging ship, then he crashed past the assassin, his fingers still probing the bloody wound in his neck. And then, with an agonized cry, he fell to the floor.

His eyes were lifeless now, his face mottled shades of red and mauve, his chest still.

The killer reached down with a gloved hand and removed the living dart. The tiny creature writhed around the assassin's finger like a putrid-green sea anemone, its twisted form flecked with crimson. The assassin placed it inside a vial, then added a few drops of the man's blood. The moss-like creature thrashed and wriggled around, splattering the vial.

The assassin leaned on its haunches and pulled out a blade. I knew what was to follow, and if I could have turned away, I would have.

I watched in mute horror as the assassin removed the man's eyes and placed them inside a pouch. It then cut a bloody gash across his throat, spilling his slow, sluggish blood. Finally it reached down and crossed the man's arms over his chest and began to whisper.

As if summoning...

...*Thump.*

The sound had come from the future.

From the spot where my empty waiting body stood in a dark apartment.

I searched frantically for a stream of time and found a blue swirl meandering towards the future. It took all of my will to drag my worn lethargic spirit from the assassin and to dive into the river of time.

The light in the apartment changed from shadows to red dawn light, before dimming back to moonlit gloom. I reached the present and slipped back inside my form. I was filled with an immediate sense of relief from the longing in my soul for this living place of warmth and familiarity. The din of my beating heart was almost deafening as I stretched, flexed my fingers, took a deep breath and...

The sound that had jarred me from the past came again.

Thump.

Someone was here, inside the apartment.

-TWELVE-

An overwhelming stench of soot and vinegar filled the air and the thump resonated again followed by the crackle of dead broken autumn leaves scraping upon a sidewalk. It was the sound of something being summoned.

I wrenched my gun from its holster.

I could feel eyes on me, watching. Cold, malicious, murderous eyes.

Something flickered on the wall. I brought my flashlight up to a painting, a vintage canvas of a glamorous woman standing on a beach, a fairground and Ferris wheel behind her. Her hairstyle and bikini were from a bygone age, and everything about the painting smacked of a longing nostalgia for a glorious time that never was.

It should have been the very picture of warmth and happiness, and yet it filled me with stone-cold dread.

And when I looked closer I saw that the woman's smile didn't quite reach her...icy green eyes. They blinked.

Someone was watching me, remotely. Using the portrait's painted eyes like a camera.

I stared back, determined not to show a shred of the fear that coiled inside me like a punch to the gut. There was a terrible darkness in those eyes, a twisted, malicious evil. "I'll find you." I leaned in close and forced a smile. "I swear it."

The eyes bored into mine and I felt a strangely familiar, powerful connection. They blinked once more before returning to their flat painted form. The watcher had gone.

I spun round as a booming hiss erupted from the kitchen, like water dropped into a pan of boiling oil.

I brought my gun up and stepped out into the hallway. My astral form had just passed this way, mere moments ago, but somehow it felt so distant.

As I rounded the doorway to the kitchen I found a molten-red pool. It spread across the scuffed linoleum floor, right where the dead man had lain with his eyeless sockets staring at the pockmarked ceiling.

That's what the assassin had been doing just before I'd been pulled back into the present. Setting a trap within the victim's blood. A trap that remained long after the gore had been scrubbed away, laying in wait for a magical presence to trigger it. The air above the bloody pool shimmered like a mirage and through it I saw a dark forest of twisted trees, their limbs bent into agonized contortions.

Someone rushed through the foliage. A man? He wore simple leather armor and long black riding boots. The top of his face was hidden behind a mask shaped like a golden barbed sun. He grinned, revealing long wolfish teeth and hissed words in a language I'd never heard before, but the sound turned my spine to ice.

A demon.

Fragrant breezes wafted up from the strange landscape, bringing a scent of pine and winter herbs. I found myself intoxicated by their cold, bitter perfume.

I'd heard plenty of tales of other worlds, but I'd never seen one. And here it was, so close. I could have stepped right into it, and I might have tried, if it hadn't been for the demon rushing toward me.

He pushed through the haze and as he stepped into the kitchen, the forest scene faded, taking the otherworldly breeze with it. Heavy black boots thundered upon the kitchen floor, spattering the spectral blood across the linoleum. He was twice my height and fire burned in his eyes as he clutched his carved knife of bone.

As I backed away he raised his blade, aimed and threw.

-THIRTEEN-

I watched hypnotized as the dagger flipped through the air.

It spun around, pommel to blade, blade to pommel in a white arc of bone.

Time seemed to slow and the sound of slicing air turned to a roar, as the demon bore down with a wide, hungry grin.

I forced myself to snap out of the spell that held me mesmerized, and ducked. The dagger struck the wall, its bone blade buried to the hilt in the plaster where I'd stood.

A demonic growl filled the room.

I fired twice, the sound almost deafening in the tight space.

Both rounds found their mark. One penetrated the leather armor, right where its heart should be. The other cracked the creature's gold mask, smack in the center. I caught a glimpse of a blackening wound and silver scales as it reached up with a long finger and slipped it into the hole. Its claws dripped with ichor as it pulled out the crumpled bullet and grimaced, its teeth gnashing in fury.

I raised my weapon to take another shot.

The demon glared at the gun, as if trying to work out what it was. As I fired, it flitted away, the bullet barely clipping its shoulder. It stormed past me in a blur of teeth, claws and silver scales.

I flinched, expecting to feel its claws tearing at my throat, but the creature made for the hallway. It was unarmed and shaken. I rushed in pursuit. It reached the front door and yanked at it. It was locked. The demon smashed its fists against the wooden panels.

I fired again, the bullet ripped a hole in its back and the demon whirled round. As it thundered towards me I fired again. The shot went wide and the creature hurtled past me, vanishing into the living room.

Smashing glass rang out and I ran down the hall to see the demon stepping through the broken window, out onto the fire escape. It gave me a final, hate-filled glare before it leapt and vanished from view.

Muffled screams and shouts echoed along the alley and startled faces gazed from windows across the street.

"Shit" The cops would be here any minute.

I grabbed a book from the floor and smashed the jagged shards of glass away from the frame before climbing out onto the fire escape.

The creature was sprawled on the ground below, its body twitching. It rolled onto its back, its piercing eyes staring up at me. Then it leapt to its feet and took off down the alley, with one hand clenched to its chest.

I flew down the fire escape, ignoring the creaks and squeals as it shook, and slid down the ladder. By the time I dropped to the ground the demon was gone. I winced at the sharp pain snapping at my ankles and hobbled on, grabbing a chunk of crystal from my bag and willing its magic to numb my pain.

When I reached the street, there was no sign of the damned creature. I grabbed a vial of Nightsight from my bag and took a swig of the acrid infusion of herbs and roots. It smelled like sewage and I was pretty sure it tasted even worse.

A tingle flickered across my eyelids and the world grew several shades darker. Soon I could see the white-hot footprints that had scorched the ground and the side of a parked car, searing its roof and the asphalt street beyond. The burning trail led over a set of iron railings and vanished beneath the wild scrub in the parkland across the street.

I winced, half blinded by the street lights as I ran across the road. The railings were hot where the creature had grabbed them so I shielded my hands as I hoisted myself up over the rusty spikes.

A jarring pain shot up my legs as I landed, and I limped along the flaming trail to where it vanished.

"Bastard."

The demon had cloaked himself.

I pulled the silver compass from my bag and its face gleamed in the moonlight as I flipped it open. Behind the glass crystal was a scattered mound of iron filings drawn to the demon's dark, eldritch power. They trembled and danced as they began to form an arrow. I followed its trail through the park towards a circle of ramshackle buildings. The remains of a small rundown amusement park. Yet another place where happiness and hope had gone to seed. What better place for a demon?

I passed a boarded-up carousel, the hoardings spray-painted with threats, promises, and territorial messages of fury, bravado and hate.

Something creaked in the darkness. I slowed as I walked past a derelict shooting gallery and raised my gun, for all the good it would do.

The filings shifted and pointed behind me...

I spun round just as the demon dropped from the gallery roof. It thudded to the ground, its heavy boots creating fissures in the asphalt.

"Who sent-" I didn't get a chance to finish before its barbed leather fist caught me under the chin. My head lurched back and my ears were filled with a riot of pain and noise.

It drew its fist back to strike me again. I dodged and its claws whistled through empty air. I grabbed its forearm and fired my gun point blank into its wrist.

The demon howled, the din stinging my ears. My nostrils flared with the sickening stench of burnt flesh and brimstone as the demon kicked out and its boot caught me in the midriff. I buckled over and the breath rushed from my lungs. I stumbled back as the creature drew its fist into the air to punch me again.

I watched as it sailed down towards me, then I grabbed it in my hand and twisted it hard. The demon howled again. I tackled it to the ground. It tried to squirm free, but I pinned it down and sat astride its chest.

I dug the hot end of the gun into the wound in its wrist. It screamed. "Hurts, does it?" I growled.

It gurgled in its alien tongue.

"Who sent you?" I pushed the gun further into the smoking hole in its wrist. Black ichor seeped from the wound and it was all I could do not to gag.

The demon shook its head as I wrenched off its mask and threw it aside, revealing an oval of silver scales. I looked into its blazing eyes. "I asked you a question."

It growled and muttered twisted, unintelligible words.

"In English." I placed the end of the gun against its forehead. "Tell me who sent you."

Its eyes grew bright. "Go to hell!"

It spat. The gob singed the side of my face. I pushed the gun harder to its skull. "I'll keep you here. You can thrash around in agony until the sun comes up and finishes you off. Is that what you want?"

"Release me." It muttered a series of words I couldn't understand.

A stabbing pain hit me with the force of a hurricane. It started in the center of my skull, as wicked as the mother of all migraines and felt as if it was singeing every one of my nerves. Most people would have caved and released the creature, but I'm not most people.

I dug into my bag with my free hand, looking for something to break the curse. A mistake. The demon seized the moment and uttered a string of sing-song words.

An invocation.

I grabbed its jaw but the flesh turned to smoke and ran through my fingers.

There was nothing I could do but watch as the demon began to dissolve. Its face rippled and blackened and my hands passed through its chest and struck the ground as the fumes filled my mouth and nostrils.

The last thing I saw was its wolfish grin and then its smoky remains snaked away on the breeze. Which seemed fitting. My whole life of late had felt like chasing smoke.

I climbed to my feet and walked away, empty handed, bruised and broken.

...

I grabbed a bottle of bourbon on the way home, the perfect companion on a slow steady one-way trip into the painless comfort of unconsciousness. I was done. No more demons, assassins or vampires. For now at least.

Storm was the only one cat in my apartment that night. I found him perched on the cabinet next to Willow's picture. Unlike the others, who only used my place as a second home, Storm was feral and lean. His shoulders were broad and hard as stone, the map of scars covering his face marked old wounds from countless battles. The first time he'd shown up was late one autumn night as lightning raged across the sky, hence his name.

I nodded to him, lit some candles and poured myself a drink. He blinked slowly back, before looking away.

The bourbon went down fast. I lay back on the sofa and gazed at the flickering flames. It had been a strange, painful day and I had almost as little to go on now, as I'd had when I'd started.

I checked my phone for updates from Haskins, but the screen was empty, so I refilled my glass, sipped it slowly and made my way to bed.

My dreams plunged me into the forest I'd seen beyond the portal. I wandered, lost among the towering, twisted trees and awoke hours later to a burning sensation on the side of my face. Right where the demon had spat at me. It still hurt like hell. I dipped my fingers in water and rubbed the spot, before attempting to pull the blanket over me.

It wouldn't move.

I gazed down at the foot of the bed to find Storm perched on the corner like a gargoyle, staring out the window.

My guardian.

I whispered a greeting to him, before falling into a long, feverish sleep.

-FOURTEEN-

My head ached and I woke with my face feeling like it had been scrubbed down with sandpaper. I reached for the glass of water on the nightstand, but it turned out to be diluted whiskey. And then I remembered the demon's spit.

"Urgh." I sat up slowly. "No," I mumbled, as if the word would stop the pain.

It didn't.

Storm was gone, most likely driven away by my drunken snores, and judging by the way my hair was standing on end, a night of thrashing around.

The world lurched as I got up and switched on the bathroom light. It fizzled and flickered like it was full of half-crazed fireflies. I splashed cold water across my face but it didn't do anything. I mean, my face and t-shirt were wet but I still felt like shit. Since I was soaked already, I decided to take a shower. I stood and swayed under hot streaming jets of water and part of the fog cleared from my mind.

The living room was cat free, but a glance at the clock confirmed it was way past their breakfast time. I felt strangely alone as I made a pot of coffee and turned the place upside down looking for my phone.

Finally I found it; stuffed down the side of the sofa along with a vintage coin and a playing card I didn't remember owning.

I thumbed the phone's display to see if there was any update from Haskins, but the battery was dead. "Out of juice," I said. "I know how you feel." I plugged the phone into the wall, grabbed my cup and slumped to the sofa, splashing boiling coffee over my knees. "Son of a bitch!" I wasn't sure if I was addressing the coffee, which was only following the dictates of gravity, or myself.

Sunlight streamed through the window and made a patch on the floor and I gazed at it as I went over my options for the day.

What did I have to go on? Nothing except the rigged murder scene and the demon that had turned to smoke. My demonologist friend Anastasia would be able to put a name to the creature that had tried to pound me to dust, but she was somewhere in Ukraine, tracking something I'd figured I'd be better off not asking too many questions about.

Which left the Organization, and that was a brick wall.

I glanced at the table. The napkin. The rune I'd drawn from Haskins' photograph. Someone would know what it meant. I just had to find the right person to ask.

But first, a *proper* cup of coffee, i.e. one that hadn't been made by me.

I started towards the door but stopped as I realized I'd rather face a whole horde of demons than deal with Mrs. Fitz in my current, aching state.

I grabbed a partially charged crystal from a wooden box on the bookshelf and used its power, along with a few stray strands of magic floating through the neighborhood. It didn't take much.

The air crackled as the power swirled around me and enchanted my clothes. Now, if Mrs. Fitz happened to open her door or glance through the peephole as I tried to sneak by, she'd see nothing but a thin shadowy smudge. She'd also experience a very strong compulsion to close her door and find something better to do.

My half-assed spell worked, and within moments I was out of the building and halfway down the street.

The sun had vanished, which was fine, the patchy gray sky matched my frayed mood. I was almost at the coffee shop when I spotted a glimmer of light and eddy of color swirling along the sidewalk across the street.

Glory.

She wore a long scarlet dress and her golden blonde hair spilled over her shoulders. Her full red lips matched her dress, which was tastefully offset by a string of pearls. She looked like an actress from the golden age of cinema, a jewel from a distant era, a Hollywood starlet of yore.

The lights and colors around her dimmed as she drew them in, leaching their brightness and adding it to her own marvelous glow. The lights shimmered and snaked towards her, as if she were a living magnet slowly turning the world monochrome.

Glory stepped into the street, draining the brilliant yellow from the cab that screeched to a halt before her. She barely gave it a glance as she walked towards me.

I was glad her eyes were hidden behind those black oversized designer shades. That way I wouldn't be drawn in. Glory was a succubus, and very dangerous when she chose to be. Not that I'd had any quarrels with her. We were friends of sorts. Most the time.

She stood before me, her pale elegant face in stark contrast to the deep dark glasses. A strange, uncomfortable silence settled over us and the world seemed drab and dim beyond her scarlet red dress.

Usually she'd greet me with an upper hook of flirtation, followed by a jab of flattery, and I'd have to fight hard to withstand the charm offensive.

But not today.

Today her flawless face was marred by the dark streaks of mascara that streamed out from beneath her glasses.

"Morning, Glory." Usually my feeble pun would put a smile on those full, plump lips, but not this time.

She stood in silence as the traffic edged past, the honking horns and muffled curses fading as her invisible aura swept around me like a tide. "Morgan." Her voice faltered.

"Are you okay?" I was worried. I was also wondering how the hell she'd found me.

"No." Her voice was almost breathless. "No, I'm not okay."

"What is it?"

Glory's breath hitched in her throat. She shook her head.

I tried another tack. "What are you doing here?"

"I walked until I caught your scent."

"My scent?" Right now it was probably a mix of sweat, bitter coffee and stale whiskey.

"Yes. I keep a kind of mental library of pheromones, mostly from people I find...interesting."

"Right. So why-"

"Tom's dead." Her voice was as cold and hard as stone.

It felt like someone had taken a sledgehammer to my chest. "Tom?"

She nodded.

"How did you know T-"

"Everyone knows...knew Tom. He looked out for people. He looked out for you. Not that he wanted you to know it." Her tears left silvery trails as they tumbled down her cheeks. She took her glasses off to wipe her eyes and I tried to look away, but it was too late.

Her eyes glistened like cut crystal. Like dappled sunlight on a stunning blue sea. But the edges were red and marred by the globs of melting mascara that still clung to her lashes.

My heart raced and a hot rush pounded in my head. Right then I would have given up every one of my deepest secrets if she'd asked.

"Sorry." Glory put her sunglasses back on. "I..."

"How did..." My voice broke. I had to swallow air before I could speak again, and when I did, it sounded like someone else's voice. "How?"

Glory's lips twisted into an ugly grimace. "Some sick bastard cut his throat and took out his eyes."

Another hammer blow.

I'd seen the exact same thing happen the night before. "Where-"

"Get them, Morgan." Glory's teeth were longer now and the illusion of beauty wore thin as a feral tone filled her voice. "That's what you do, right? You get bad people."

I nodded dumbly. Molten bile scorched my throat. I wanted to throw up.

"And when you get them," Glory placed a hand on my arm, her nails digging into my arm, "make them suffer. Make them really suffer. Promise me you'll do that."

"I will." The world spun and the only thing grounding me to reality was the bite of her nails as they dug into my skin.

"Good. Tear out their fucking heart, Morgan. I'd do it myself if I knew how to find them."

The world stopped lurching around me. The hangover was gone. Ice filled my veins. I'd been here before, with Willow. Another sickening death. Another debt to be collected. "Leave it to me."

Glory gave a slight incline of her head, which I took to be an agreement. "Just get them, Morgan. Promise me."

"I will, I swear it. Where did it happen?"

Glory gave me details of an underpass near the waterfront. It was in the middle of nowhere. I wondered what had driven Tom out there.

"The place is swarming with cops," Glory said. I thought of Haskins. My phone should be charged by now. "And..." Glory continued, and stopped.

"And what?"

"There was someone there. A man. He wore a hat and his face was all shadow. I don't know what he was, and I don't want to. But he wasn't the killer, I know that much. I couldn't smell blood on him, but I could smell...I don't know. It was like madness. Barely contained madness."

I thought back to the Organization and my visit to the offices the day before. That man with the hat, was he looking for this killer too? I shivered.

Glory squeezed my arm. "Morgan. Make them pay."

"I will."

Glory turned and crossed the street and cut through the rushing river of steel, glass and rust without a care. And then she turned the corner at the end of the block and was gone.

My fury uncoiled like a reel of barbed wire. Moments later it was eclipsed by a flood of grief, helplessness and self-blame.

I'd let Tom down.

The walk back to the apartment felt hollow and desolate. I vaguely heard Mrs. Fitz emerge from her apartment as I'd walked past, climbed the stairs and slammed the door on the world.

-FIFTEEN-

I sat and stared through the window without really seeing anything, frozen by a cocktail of guilt and grief. Guilt for my failure to catch the killer and the shroud of grief for Tom's passing. I'd tried to warn him but he'd pushed me away. There had been so little to go on, no leads, even less time. But I couldn't shake the guilt. I should have been able to protect him.

It seemed strange to grieve for someone I'd barely known. A man whose past was as blank as mine and whose ambitions and hopes were just as unknown to me as the reason he'd ended up on the streets in the first place.

Dark clouds rolled over the city, bringing fat lazy drops of rain. I watched them fall as I tried to summon the will to move, to break free.

Soon anger gave me the strength to stand. I dialed Haskins and grilled him. By the end of our heated conversation, I was still at square one. All he could tell me was that forensics had concluded the two murders were almost certainly done by the same hand and that Tom was in a body bag at the city morgue. Poor Tom, waiting on a gurney in a long line of Jane and John Doe's until the Organization whisked him away.

I poured another cup of bitter black coffee, topping it off with whiskey for good measure. Time was mine to kill. I couldn't just head out to the crime scene in broad daylight. So I checked through my bag, refilled my kit, and made a bowl of pasta. I even managed to eat a good third of it before chucking the rest into the trash.

Then, with the alarm set, I closed my eyes and waited for night to fall.

...

The underpass where Tom's body had been found was surrounded by a desolate railyard filled with decaying train cars. They stood like great rusting caterpillars mottled with neon graffiti and the weedy gravel beneath them glittered with tiny squares of glass.

Clumps of turf and brush ran alongside the waterfront, waylaid in places by a potholed path. A cold breeze rose from the water, carrying a damp scent that mingled with the greasy odor of industrial decay. It was a haunted place, plagued by its past. A casualty of boom years gone bust. I could almost feel the presence of the working men and women that had once thrived here, now long since gone to their graves.

Why had Tom come here? Had he been chased, or coaxed? Either way, it was such a cold, forlorn place to die.

The underpass loomed ahead, a black circle in the side of a grassy bank crested by train tracks. There were fresh marks and debris in the dirt; car tires, footprints, cigarette butts and broken polystyrene cups. I thought of Haskins. He'd been here, his little black book in hand as he pored over Tom's corpse like it was some kind of specimen.

Not that I blamed him. It wasn't his fault or the fault of the police, it was just the way of the world. There was little that could be done to stop people like Tom from dying. Sometimes people just lost their way. Slipped through the cracks of a society they'd never quite fitted into.

The lost, the forgotten.

A scrap of police tape snapped in the breeze like a yellow serpent as I paused before the tunnel's entrance. I could barely see the end but for a dim half circle of light that defined the silhouettes of burnt-out cars amid the gulf of darkness.

The eerie solitude exploded with noise and light as a train rattled overhead, taking its passengers to brighter, happier places.

I held the collar of my coat over my mouth as I entered the tunnel. An inadequate shield against the pungent stench of piss that assailed my nostrils. I flipped on my flashlight and followed the scores of footprints.

Cops, coroners, forensics and somewhere, Tom's.

And his attacker's.

Something scuttled in the gloom. Probably a rat. The usual junk littered the ground; broken bottles, crumpled brown bags, discarded syringes, and a wealth of bent and punctured cans. I shone the flashlight over walls marred by decades of graffiti, the cobwebs and filth slowly obscuring the names and tags of yesteryear.

Why had Tom come here? Sure he was a drunk, and the place probably made a good shelter while sinking bottles of cheap vodka, but this wasn't his style.

No, something had lured him here. Panic? Terror?

I needed to take a closer look.

I held a pair of crystals in my hand and absorbed their magic, before drifting out of myself and slipping through the whirls and eddies of time. The scene changed. Beams of lights filled the tunnel, illuminating the police forensics team in their white uniforms as they searched the ground. Detectives flashed lights over the rusted cars and scoured every inch of the place.

One beam found the body slumped against the tunnel wall.

Tom.

His hair was wild around his shoulders, its grey and white tips stained red. A wide gash split his throat and caked it with congealed blood. His eyes were gone, the sockets pools of red-black, his ashen hands folded over his chest.

As if he were sleeping.

I looked for another whirl of time to take me further back.

I saw a rookie cop entering the tunnel, the flashlight in his hand trembling, a couple of kids on mountain bikes following behind him. I went further back, until I saw the same kids cycling through the gloom, their laughs and jeers turning to screams that echoed beneath the sloping roof.

I went back further still, the tunnel was empty. Tom entered, carrying what looked like a short sword. He walked backwards, his eyes narrowed as he glared towards the tunnel's entrance, his back straight, his fear hidden. But I could still sense the steady racing thump of his heart.

Then a figure appeared. It was the assassin, its step slow. Confident. Predatory.

I swooped down to meld with its form. I wanted to learn more about my enemy but its thoughts were just as limited as before.

Then I heard the whispering in the center of its mind.

Kill.

The force and coldness of the words shook me from my mooring, and I was thrown from the assassin.

I watched as it pulled a sword from its cloak. The blade was smooth, polished and as black as onyx. The bleached bone pommel was visible beneath its iron-like grip, and it had been carved into the shape of a skull. Symbols were etched along the blade and while I could not discern their meaning, they felt distantly familiar.

Tom stopped, stood his ground and with one hand he buttoned up his coat.

It was a smooth cool action but it seemed a strange thing to do. Then the thought was snatched away as he called out, "Who's here with you?"

For a moment I thought he meant me, but then he added, "Who commands you? Who pulls your strings?"

The assassin ignored him as it strode forward and brought up its blade. Its head cocked and twitched as if listening to the whispering voice inside its mind. And then it spoke. "Cowardice. Dishonor. Weakness," it said in a hoarse, lifeless voice.

Tom gripped his sword. "Who are you?"

"Sleep, old man. Sleep like those you slaughtered."

Tom's sword gleamed as he leaped forward. A feint white glow illuminated the blade as he swung it through the air.

The assassin parried it, then jumped forward to meet him and landed a hard punch to his face. Tom's nose exploded with blood, but he barely seemed to register it as he jumped back and slashed forward.

The assassin slammed its sword into Tom's and drove him back. It lunged, thrusting the dark blade at Tom's heart. It struck his coat. The fabric shimmered with bright blue light and the sword juddered and sang, as if it had struck stone.

Tom swung his blade, opening a deep cut across the assassin's midriff. It showed no reaction as it shouldered him back and brought its knee up into his groin. Tom buckled over, his face a mask of agony.

The assassin raised its blade for the killing blow, but shuddered as Tom drove his sword through its chest. The creature grabbed the blade in its gloved hand and plunged it in deeper, wrenching it from Tom's grasp.

Tom stared in open eyed amazement and horror, then recognition dawned across his ravaged face. "You're..."

He never finished his words. The assassin wrenched the sword from its chest and swung it in elaborate arcs through the air, leaving a deep red line across Tom's throat.

Agony and bewilderment filled Tom's eyes as he threw a hand up, trying to stem the wound. Blood gushed between his knuckles and his eyes grew wide.

The assassin sheathed its blade, shoved Tom's weapon into the dirt and reached down, pulling Tom's hand away from the lethal gash. Blood misted the air and spattered the heap of rusted cars behind him.

Tom let out a final gasp while the assassin stood over him, muttering in a language both alien and hauntingly familiar. And then he slumped to the ground, dead.

The assassin turned him over onto his back and widened the gash in his throat, before pulling a knife from its belt and leaning over to remove his eyes.

I refused to look away, even though I knew that nothing could ever erase this horror. It would live on in my mind, forever...no matter how many bottles of whiskey I sank.

When it had finished, the assassin stood up and left the tunnel.

I should have pursued it but the magic was wearing off, leaving me feeling stretched and thin. I hung in the air as I searched for a way back. Eddies of time swirled around me like wisps of emerald green and midnight blue clouds and I spotted a current drifting back to the present and dove in.

Night turned to dawn and day, and finally back to night. I could see my body, the flashlight in my hand, the illuminated patch of dirt still wet with Tom's blood.

I drifted down and anchored myself, my body as warm as a summer evening. I waited, trying to ground myself before walking out of the tunnel, but my thoughts flew wildly, like a flock of starlings. All wings and claws turning in a spiral of sorrow and fury.

-SIXTEEN-

That night my dreams carried me to a great hill forested with oak, ash and tall thick trees of a name I couldn't recall. Their boughs were wide and twisted with pale bark and delicate papery leaves.

A spired city rose up from the valley below, its walls and domes hewn from amber stone that glittered in shades of coral and peach as the sun set. At the city's center was a grand palace with fountains and pools that reflected the vast crimson sky.

I knew this city well. I'd explored its labyrinthine streets for most of my early adulthood. It had been a home for a while, but now it was dangerous, a place of shadows and doubt, the citizens stalked by suspicion and fear. A range of black, brittle mountains framed the city like an ominous backdrop, streaks of bloody red sunlight spilling between their shards and peaks.

"We need to go." The man's voice was gruff, familiar.

I turned, but his face was a swarm of movement and I could not discern his features. "I can't see you." My young voice cracked with terror.

"You must forsake this world. It's the only way you'll survive."

Branches snapped as a line of soldiers moved up the hill toward us, sunlight glinting on the swords in their hands.

They did not look like men. Their helmets were long and silver. Almost wolf like.

"Quick." A gentle calloused hand grabbed my wrist and led me away. We ran through the trees and crashed through the heavy brush. My heart beat hard with fear and anger. Part of me wanted to turn back, fight, slay every single one of our pursuers, but I couldn't. I was just a child.

"Faster!" The man pulled me through the undergrowth until we emerged in a small clearing that led to a cavern in the side of a hill. The darkened opening buzzed and flickered. The sight of it filled me with nausea and panic.

This was a mystical place steeped in folklore and legend.

The cave at the end of the world where those who entered never returned.

"Come." The faceless man pulled me on. "We have to go. We'll die if we're captured. I swear, if there was another way..."

I tried to squirm free. I flailed my arms and grabbed a branch but its mossy coating was slick and it slipped from my fingers as the man yanked my arm and dragged me to the cave.

Shouts echoed through the trees.

The man ran on. Arrows whizzed past us and smashed against the rock face. "The Gods help us," he cried as the gaping black void rushed towards us. Then his voice was snatched away by the sound of a roaring, churning sea. The last thing I saw as the darkness swept us away was the golden glimmer of the ring on his hand.

It was Tom's.

-SEVENTEEN-

I sat up drenched in sweat, my dreams lingering and my heart pounding. It took a few moments to remember where I was and then a few more to ground myself.

Back on earth. It was a strange thought, and yet I knew it was true. The dreams had taken me somewhere else, to memories of a far off world.

A realm that couldn't be, and yet was. Were the dreams memories, or figments from my fevered imagination? Was I having another breakdown? Had the insanity and evil overwhelming the city finally gotten to me too?

My terror of madness was never far away, I'd borne it silently for as long as I could remember. Willow had known, but the wildness of her world made mine seem tame by comparison.

I'd told her everything one drunken night. Of plunging through a sea of black only to find myself in abandoned asylum, with a man whose face I couldn't see. Of waking, with no memories, into my body aged ten.

She'd given me an unreadable, bittersweet smile, and then she'd filled our glasses with wine and proposed a toast. "To life in all its beauty and madness."

"To life in all its beauty and madness," I said, as I rolled out of the tangled blankets and wandered into the living room. Two cats stared at each other from across the apartment, one on top of the television, the other on the bookcase. They watched with expectant, gluttonous eyes as I opened the fridge. There was nothing inside but the flickering light, a takeout container of something I'd long forgotten, half a tin of tuna and a lone can of beer. "Sad bastard," I muttered. "I need to sort my life out."

I sat and gazed at the napkin on the table, the one from Nika's Diner. Unfinished business. The killer was still at large and I had no idea how to find it. I knew next to nothing other than it was some kind of remotely operated, half-living automaton.

A flesh and blood drone, a golem.

The only real lead I had was the scar-like rune carved on Tom and the other victim, and I needed to find out what in the hell it meant.

I fed the cats and called Haskins but he had no news, so I hung up and headed for the shower, hoping the water would clear my foggy mind.

It did, a little. I threw on some clothes, grabbed my phone and headed out.

...

"Books, Nooks, Oddments and Glamours" was a suitably tatty occult store situated halfway down Nightfall Street. The street itself was little more than a long dark thoroughfare with alleys that ran off it like the branches of a great sprawling tree.

As with most of the more magical places in the city, Nightfall Street was rarely visited by anyone non-magical, even though it was within walking distance of the heart of the city.

Anyone who somehow managed to wander unbidden within its thoroughfares would soon find themselves with a heavy sense of melancholy and an urgent need to be as far away as possible. To be back in the real world of drama and chatter, debt and banks, and mountains of highly priced crap that nobody needed.

The day was overcast and shadows gathered below the shop awnings and seeped from the tightly packed alleyways. I wove through the milling tangles of shoppers, their faces obscured by hats and hoods. They clutched bags at their sides, jealously guarding their purchases. Which were most likely ingredients or enchantments they'd bought to patch the weaknesses in their own craft and make their sorcery harder to counter. A good motivation for secrecy.

I turned into the short passage that led to Books, Oddments and Glamours and slowed as I spotted three figures gathered in the gloom. Their hoods were low over their faces, but I caught enough of their ashen pallor to see they were vampires. They passed a joint of rare and magical herbs between them and grinned, revealing long teeth.

Their smiles faded when they clapped eyes on me.

They turned to face me, reflecting the grey sky in their round rimless shades. One hissed to the others, his thin lips twisting into a hard, mocking scowl.

Associates of the late Mr. Tudor? It was more than possible. News of his untimely demise must have broken by now and vampires were surprisingly loyal.

They blocked the shop door as I approached and only then did I realize I was completely unarmed, I'd left my gun and bag of tricks back at home. I didn't let that stop me, I walked right up to the nearest and leaned in close until our noses were almost touching. "Boo!"

He moved.

Just a fraction.

It was enough. I shoved them out of my way, pushed the shop door open, and the bells inside chimed in a twinkling arpeggio.

A heady scent of incense filled my nose, amber, cedar wood, musk and myrrh. And dust. Lots and lots of dust.

I passed dark rows of bookshelves and tables overflowing with candles, pouches, crystals and wands. I noticed a new display and a large bright yellow cardboard box stuffed full of vials of pick-me-up charms. I was fairly sure it was hokum but couldn't help but be intrigued by its claim of 'Four hours of non-stop Zest and Shine'.

"You don't need that." Talulah Feist stood between a pair of red velvet curtains, a large notebook in her hand. "You already shine like an evening star, Morgan Rook." She smiled then glanced over a tray of rainbow-colored orbs and scribbled in her ledger. "I hate doing inventory even more than I hate Tuesdays." She flicked an imaginary piece of fluff from her simple yet sleek cream colored wrap dress. It perfectly complemented the magenta highlights in her long brown hair, as well as the large pearl-grey eyes that flashed behind her heavy black horn-rimmed glasses. "And what brings you to my fabulous shop?"

"Questions."

Tallulah swept a hand towards the aisles of books. "Go forth and seek your answers." Her smile wavered as the door flew open behind me, filling the shop with a peal of chimes. I turned but could see no one. I was about to ask Tallulah who it had been, when she glanced down at the phone in my hand and her face fell. "Must you bring that damnable device into my emporium?"

I flipped through the photos and pulled up a picture of the rune I'd sketched of the carving on the first victim's arm. "Do you know what this means?"

"Maybe. But..." Her brow furrowed, "but I'm not sure where I've seen it. Let me dig around a bit." Talulah leafed through the pages of her notebook and made a quick sketch of the symbol. "Anything to break the monotony of this hideous inventory. Wait here."

I wandered towards the rows of bookcases and browsed until a particularly fat dusty tome caught my eye. It was filled with neat, slanted handwritten words but I was not familiar with the language. I shivered as the book began to grow heavy and cold, and quickly slipped it back onto the shelf.

The shop grew darker as I wandered further down the aisle and the dim light from the string of tiny bulbs flickered. The gloom at the end was as thick as syrup, but I saw someone move within the darkness and I caught a flash of eyes.

And then I heard a footstep behind me.

I spun round to find a hooded vampire bearing down on me, fangs out, a curved blade clenched in his fingers. I kept my eyes trained on his hand and waited for him to make his move.

And then I heard a rustle behind me.

Both his associates swept from the murk, their pale faces twisted with murderous hate.

-EIGHTEEN-

I leaned back as the vampire's blade whizzed less than an inch from my face. "Piece of shit," he spat.

I glanced from him to the others, gauging their positions, before turning back to him. "You've been alive how long? Centuries?" I asked, looking to buy time, "And that's the extent of your vocabulary?"

"Go to hell!" He sprang forward and lunged at my throat. I grabbed a book from the shelf to block the knife. The blade pierced the cover, sank clean through the pages, and gleamed as it emerged from the leather backing. The book let out a piercing wail and its pages began to glow. I pulled it towards me, wrenching the blade from the vampire's grip and threw the impaled shuddering tome to the floor, as a pale sinewy arm slipped over my shoulder from behind. One of his friends had me in a headlock and his clawed fingers reached for my eyes.

I thrust my elbow back as hard as I could.

I struck the vampire with a sickening crunch. As I drew forward for a second blow, it vanished.

The vampire ahead lunged, his teeth drawn back. I punched him hard above the eye and felt my ring cut through his papery skin.

Blood dripped into his eye, slowing him.

I spun back around and threw a jab at the third vampire as he tried to grab me. He came apart in a cloud of black motes that fluttered in the air like moths.

I broke through the ashy haze just as one of the vampires raised a gun.

Light flashed and an explosion echoed through the shop. I flinched, expecting to feel searing red hot pain, but the bullet struck the book beside my head.

A fresh cloud of motes appeared, black and magenta, they swirled into a human silhouette and within the blink of an eye Tallulah appeared. She shoved me aside and bore down on the pair of vampires stalking behind me. Her fangs were fully exposed and far longer than theirs, the bloodlust in her eyes much keener.

They fell back.

Tallulah seized the closest one. "You come into my shop..." She grabbed his arm and wrenched it behind his back with a terrible snapping sound. "...and destroy my books."

A high-pitched scream added to the whine in my ears.

"And cry like a little girl!" Tallulah was a blaze of motion as she threw the vampire to the ground and whirled back to confront the next one. She seized his gun and threw it into the shadows before pulling the vampire's fingers hard. The crack that followed made me wince.

"You harass my friend..." Tallulah growled, before vanishing and reappearing as the final vampire tried to flee from the aisle. She blocked his path and stood firm as he hissed and lunged at her. Her porcelain hand shot out and seized him by the neck, then she turned his head back and gave his throat a savage bite.

A fine spray of blood misted the air, coating the books in a red haze. He howled and tried to squirm free.

"I should take all three of you to the cellar and feed you to my brood."

"Please." The vampire whimpered. Tallulah released him. He scuttled off to join the others as they backed away down the aisle.

"Please," Tallulah repeated. "That's better. You have some manners after all. Now get out of my shop before I eviscerate all three of you."

They burst into clouds of black and red smoke, and raced away. Bells tinkled and the front door thumped closed behind them.

Tallulah transformed back to her former appearance and even though the unbridled savagery was gone there was still a tinge of wildness in her eyes. "The book you used as a shield is probably worth more than you earn in a year."

"I'm sorry," I said. And I was.

Tallulah nodded. "Of course you are. And while sorry is nice, it's never going to replace my book. Which means you owe me a favor. *Another* favor."

"Sure." There were worse people to be indebted to. "Whatever I can do."

Tallulah gave me a hungry smile and guided me down the aisle. The cold chill of her hand sunk through my coat as she clasped my shoulder. "Your list of enemies grows by the day, Morgan."

"That's just part of the job."

Her sardonic smile faded. "I heard about Mr. Tudor."

"Word spreads fast." I swallowed, hoping she hadn't taken his death personally.

"He was connected to some very bad people," she shrugged. "Which is probably why those lowlifes gave you such a warm welcome. And now I've been drawn into the whole sordid affair."

"My apologies."

"Why aren't you armed? You should have a weapon with you at all times. You shouldn't need me to tell you that."

I didn't. But the last couple of days had kicked the shit out of me. I nodded. "I know."

"The Crimson Eye won't rest. They're relentless. They'll come after you and they're not going to stop until you wipe them out."

I knew that too. But I had bigger fish to fry and this was no time to worry about a low level coven of vampires. "I had to stop Tudor, he gave me no choice. He went off the synthetic, started picking up innocents and mainlining them."

"Innocents?" Tallulah laughed. "Neither of our worlds have much in the way of innocents these days, do they? Still, we have rules and they must be abided by. For now at least."

We strolled down the gloomy aisle toward the front of the shop and I was glad for the light and the window, as dusty and streaked with soot as it was. "For now?"

"The treaty, it's just words and good intentions. Words and intentions change, and change is coming. I wonder how long the agreements will hold."

The thought had crossed my mind too. "About that symbol..."

Tallulah's nail broke my skin as she placed her finger on my lip. "I'll tell you what I know, but I want no further part in this business. Do you understand?"

"Sure."

"Good. Do you know Argyle Screed?"

"The merchant? I know of him." Argyle Screed was a person of interest to the Organization, but there were plenty of others in the line ahead of him.

"I had dealings with Screed a few months back when he sold me some rare, forbidden books. You're probably aware his business can get a little dangerous at times, hence his need to hire mercenaries. There was a new one with him when we last met, a woman. She was wearing long sleeves but I saw that symbol you just showed me peeking out from below her cuff."

"Do you know where I can find her?"

"No, you'll have to ask him."

I needed to visit a lowlife like Screed like I needed salmonella."Where can I find him?" People like Argyle Screed tended to move about a lot.

"I've heard there's an underground in a bar on Silversmith Street. You might want to look there. It's called the-"

"The Seventh Knot. I know it."

"Be sure to arm yourself this time."

"I will." I was about to leave when Tallulah leaned over and kissed the side of my face. I suppressed a flinch as I felt her attention stray to the side of my neck.

"Remember your debt to me, Morgan Rook," she called, as I pulled the door open and filled the shop with a cold breeze. I nodded, closed the door behind me and stepped out into the alley.

I'd almost made it to Nightfall Street when someone clapped a hand on my shoulder and pulled me back into the shadows.

-NINETEEN-

My hand automatically lurched toward my holster, the one that wasn't there.

"A word, Morgan."

The silken yet husky tone was unmistakable. Underwood. He stood in the shadows behind me as impeccably dressed as ever. His sharp charcoal grey coat with that freshly pressed cream colored shirt and the black silk tie made me feel like a bum.

His fedora was tipped at an angle over his long pale face, emphasizing the glint of his lilac eyes as he gave me a tired half-smile. "You've been busy." Underwood glanced at the wealth of cuts and bruises on the side of my face. "Despite my request for you to stay out of it."

"I-"

"Not here." Underwood glanced around. "Somewhere private." Fury simmered below his polite, cordial tone as he led me down the alley past a number of seedy shops and bars. Figures gathered outside the doorways. I knew I was unlikely to run into trouble, especially with Underwood by my side, but I assessed them out of habit; the large woman that must have been part giantess, a pale, ratty-faced sorcerer and a group of twitchy addicts with bright roving eyes. Their gaze grew hungry as they glanced our way, but no one bothered us.

We walked in silence, then Underwood guided me down an unmarked alley I'd never noticed before. He stopped in front of a heavy arched metal door with a facade of golden filigree and fed a dull silver key into the lock. "After you," he said, as he opened the door.

The air inside was inviting, warm and fragrant with roasting meats, fresh bread, sautéed onions, the bouquets of spices that were familiar, and some that were not. My mouth watered and I realized I couldn't remember the last time I'd eaten.

Underwood locked the door and led me down a flight of plum-colored carpeted stairs. Twinkling music rang out in a delicate melody played by something that sounded like a cross between a mandolin and a harp.

The dining room at the foot of the stairs was long and wide, the formal tables were tucked into a series of nooks and the large central space was occupied by an ornate marble fountain carved into the form of classical sylvan riverside. Stone dryads frolicked in the stream and basked in the water cascading from the mouth of a giant copper fish.

A maître d' approached us. He was smartly dressed in black and white and his eyes were the color of honey. They scanned me, fast, judging, unimpressed, but they gleamed as they found Underwood. "The usual, Mr. Underwood?"

"Yes. And a..." Underwood's brow furrowed as he glanced at me. "And a pint of stout for my friend. It's too early for bourbon."

The maître d' led us to the far end of the room. We passed nooks filled with diners, their conversations low and impossible to hear. I recognized one; a notorious dealer of arcane art, and I noticed the two ladies sitting with him were both cloaked lycanthropes. A female demon sat in the next alcove reading quietly on a tablet as she sipped from a delicate glass filled with bright blue fire.

The maître d' paused.

"Sit." Underwood gestured to a table enclosed by ornate mahogany walls and an intricately carved ceiling. A formal scarlet tablecloth embroidered with gold thread set off the elegantly trimmed china and fine linen napkins that had been folded into the shape of white swans.

There were no menus.

Underwood sat in the far corner, and I took the seat opposite him, feeling like a naughty schoolboy waiting for the lecture to begin. He sat in silence and only once our drinks arrived, his a glass of dark red wine, did he speak.

"I thought we had an understanding, Morgan. I assign a job, you complete the task, I compensate you. Granted the pay's low, especially considering the risks. But we work with what we have and the Organization doesn't have much." He took a deep breath and spread his ringed fingers against the tablecloth. "Now, despite the courtesy I've always shown you, you've chosen to defy me. Why?"

"It's not that simple-"

"But it is. I told you to stay out of this business, and you didn't." Underwood gave me a long, hard look. "I heard an off-world demon was raised. You know the penalty for such deeds, seeing as you enforce them." His almond-shaped eyes narrowed as he took another sip of his drink.

"You know I didn't raise that demon."

"Maybe. But I have witnesses that put you at the scene. Yours aren't the only eyes I have in the city. Not by a long shot."

"The place was rigged. Someone set a trap. The demon would have been triggered by any magical presence it detected. I chased it down, it self-destructed, end of story."

Underwood's gaze locked on to mine. "You mentioned a friend, one who had the same markings as the first victim. I assume that's what drove you to the crime scene."

My words caught in my throat. I nodded.

Fleeting pity passed through Underwood's eyes, and then they hardened. "You know I'm not one for repeating myself or wasting my time, or anyone else's. So let me cut to the quick. I understand your particular interest in these crimes, Morgan, but I told you to leave it to the Organization. That order still stands."

I took a heavy sip of stout, glad for the liquid courage. While I wasn't frightened of Underwood, I was definitely wary. I'd heard stories about people who had crossed him, none of them came off the better for it. "Why?"

"I've already explained, the matter's being dealt with."

"By who?" I matched his stare.

"By our *betters*." There was both irony and resignation in his voice.

"Meaning the Council."

"We're just pawns," Underwood continued. "The little people. Which makes the magical world no different to the human one. There are hierarchies in both, pecking orders, kings, king-makers and peasants. Law and order, chaos and disorder. Our job is merely to keep things in check. To prevent the occult from being seen. To ensure *they* remain unaware of our presence in their world, and in doing so, thus far, we've prevented a bloodbath of biblical proportions."

"By *they* I take it you mean humans. You seem to forget I'm one myself."

Underwood's laugh was short and hard. "You're more us than them. Even though I often suspect you wish that wasn't so."

He was right. The idea of a normal life free from constant conflict and turmoil was appealing. A life where I was only judged by banal details like my bank balance and social status, rather than my prowess or grasp of magic, or lack of. "So the Council's overseeing the investigation? They don't usually show this much interest in our affairs. What's so different about these killings?"

"You know we don't talk about the Council, Morgan. You work for the Organization, not them. At least not directly. That's all you need to know"

Right. The Organization being the iron fist to the Council's supposed velvet glove of learnedness, justice and order. "All I need to know," my voice grew louder but I didn't care, "is who killed my friend. And how to find them so I can wipe them out as slowly and painfully as possible. That's all."

Underwood finished his drink and set the glass down. "I don't make the rules, I'm just an intermediary. My remit was very clear. Stay away from this case and leave it to my esteemed partners to deal with."

"So they can pass it on to agents like Raspailkin, Ebomee and Osbert?" I shook my head in disgust. "Each of which is a hair's breadth away from being the kind of scum we hunt down."

"Scum or not, they know how to follow orders and maintain professionalism in their work."

I snorted.

"Don't push me, Morgan. Take a holiday. Go somewhere warm. Or go somewhere cold if you prefer. Whatever suits you. Just go away and stay out of this business." Underwood put cash on the table, more than enough to cover the check and leave a very generous tip, then he stood. "Stay, have a few more drinks. Toast your departed friend or drown your sorrows. It's on me."

He began to walk away, but stopped. "Do what I tell you, Morgan, and maybe we'll both survive to fight another day."

I sipped the rest of my pint as I waited for him to leave, then I got up. I didn't feel too steady on my feet; the beatings, pain and stress of the last few days had begun to take their toll. The waiter watched me with a look of displeasure and someone in one of the nooks laughed as I passed by.

I didn't care. They could all go to hell.

I had places to be, and monsters to see.

-TWENTY-

I was glad to get away from Nightfall Street, to be back in my world. Glad to be home. I loaded my gun and double checked my kit. I had enough crystals, to keep me going for at least a few more encounters, but I'd be needing more, and soon.

My head swam with exhaustion. I took a cold shower, changed into my work clothes; a black sweater, jeans and boots, and made myself an even blacker cup of coffee.

It was time to find the notoriously slippery Argyle Screed. From what little I knew, he moved around a lot, but mostly operated out of a dive on the wharf. Screed was never far from the water, as allegedly most of his trade was smuggled in aboard nocturnal ships.

I had no specifics on exactly what that trade was. There were rumors, exotic forbidden spices, rare magical artifacts, even people. All of which should have placed him high on the Organization's priority list, but he wasn't. Whether this was down to bribes or blackmailing of high level officials, namely the Council, was pure speculation.

The prospect of going to the wharf wasn't a happy one. I had no idea what I'd find there, but I was fairly sure it wasn't going to be high tea. The whole area brimmed with lowlifes, and there was a good chance I'd encounter people and entities I'd already crossed swords with. Old enemies.

I locked the apartment and headed for the stairs, keeping to the shadows as I slipped by Mrs. Fitz's apartment. I'd almost made it when I heard the telltale *click.*

Her door opened wide, spilling light across the hall and illuminated my foot before I could yank it back into the darkness. "Why are you lurking, Mr. Rook?" Mrs. Fitz's pince-nez glasses flashed as she gazed at me. "And where have you been?"

"I've been pretty busy-"

"Did you hear them?"

"Hear who?"

Mrs. Fitz shook her head. "The cats! Who else? They were tramping across the ceiling like furry trolls dancing the two-step at some macabre ball." She narrowed her eyes. "But I must have imagined it, mustn't I?"

"You must have. I don't own cats." It was true. Kind of. I didn't own cats because, like most human slaves to the feline empire, they owned me. "Look, I-"

"I had another dream, Mr. Rook. It was horrible." Mrs. Fitz sighed. "Dreadful."

"What happened?"

She pursed her lips. "The pale man. He was in a huge dark... building...a place of great suffering. There was a room at the top of the stairs, and cells with people screaming and whimpering as devils tormented them. He stood at the threshold of the turmoil and even though he had his back to me, I could see well enough that he was gathering shadows in the palms of his pale hands."

"Gathering shadows?"

"Yes. He held his hands under a fountain of shadows, they flowed into his palms, and made him stronger. I could see it all so clearly. I tried to get away but my feet were stuck rigid, and then he turned..." The fear in Mrs. Fitz's eyes became guilt as she added, "It was you, Morgan. And then you whispered."

"Whispered what?"

"*Go to sleep.* And that was when I woke."

"I see," I said. Even though I really didn't. But once again I felt as if Mrs. Fitz's dreams were gnawing at my psyche like a dog with a rancid old bone.

"You were the painted man." Her tone was almost accusatory.

"It was just a dream, Mrs. Fitz. Forget it."

"I'll never forget it. Never." She shook her head, before giving me a weak smile. "I'm sorry, Mr. Rook. You don't want to hear my stuff and nonsense. I'll bid you a good evening." Mrs. Fitz shivered as she softly closed her door.

Her dream left me feeling unsettled.

Go to sleep.

Was it a figment of her imagination, or something more? Tudor's words came back to me.

The city's going to hell, the ones who have kept to the shadows are venturing out. Taking what they want.

Was the painted man one of those in the shadows? Was he now venturing out?

I hurried out the front door, into a chill breeze. Now wasn't the time for reflection.

Now was the time for action.

...

The Seventh Knot was a sprawling tavern on the wharf. It catered exclusively to the magical and occult communities, which made me one of the very few *blinkered* people to have even noticed its existence.

I stopped in a shadowy alcove and checked my gun for what must have been the third or fourth time. I hoped I wouldn't need it, but this area was definitely one of the more lawless places in the city, a regular Wild West.

The rickety door to the Seventh Knot was covered in stains of dubious origins, not to mention scuffs, dents, and splatters of blood. A din rose from within, cackling laughter punctured the low buzz of conversation and the heavy drone of a band that sounded like Black Sabbath but wasn't.

I walked through the door as if I'd been drinking there my whole life. The rough floorboards smelt of citrus and detergent with a heady undercurrent of blood and vomit. Nice.

Round tables filled the barroom, but most of the clientele sat on the outskirts, tucked into the shadows. I spotted a few humans, at first glance at least, as well as a witch sitting with an ogre.

A few heads turned my way, mostly from a group of wild-haired men in the back corner. They wore black leather jackets with flaming eyes painted on the shoulders.

The Sons of Hades - a notorious biker gang of vampires and half demons. I recognized the one holding court at the foot of the table, a grizzled bear of a man called Dubois. He glared daggers at me.

Or should I say, glared a *dagger,* as his right eye, which looked like a cloudy blue marble, was completely sightless. I'd sent his brother to Stardim a few years back for the attempted consumption of a minor, but not before beating him to a quivering pulp.

Dubois's hand slipped inside his jacket. I flashed a smile, my own hand resting on the grip of my revolver. He stared at me for a moment longer, then turned his attention back to his acolytes and his beer.

The long wide bar was tended by a gaunt young punk with a radiant teal mohawk and innumerable piercings that flashed in the light. I wondered if he had any concept of how badly the brightly colored booze in the bottles behind him clashed with his hair.

"What can I get you?" His plastic smile didn't quite reach his flint-hard eyes.

"I'm looking for Argyle Screed."

"There's no one here by that name."

I stared hard at him.

He blinked. "But if there was," he continued, "who would I say was looking for him?"

"That was clumsy." I didn't like this man at all. I felt like I could almost smell his soul, and it was rotten to the core. "Just tell me where Screed is."

He put his hair-spray through its paces as he shook his head. "You should leave."

I ignored the sticky patch on the bar as I leaned in, my face inches from his. "And you should direct me to Screed, before I lose what's left of my patience."

He muttered and began to wipe a pint glass with a limp filthy rag, adding more dirt than he took off. I reached over, grabbed his shirt and reeled him in like a fish.

"Get the-" He froze as I opened my other hand and blew a scattering of powder into his face.

The effect was instantaneous. Horror clouded his eyes, and his hands began to tremble.

I released him as I heard movement behind me. Two of the braver members of The Sons of Hades were right at my back. Vampires...so much for that useless mirror at the back of the bar. Light glinted on the spiked knuckleduster encasing the closest's one's fingers.

"Finish your drinks, and get the hell out of here." I pulled my gun out. They looked at each other, before making the right decision.

I turned back. The barkeeper was shaking uncontrollably as the hexdust and nightshade mix took him into his own personal hell. I slipped a hand into my pocket, charged up with the chunk of crystal, and closed my eyes before slipping into his mind.

It was awash with black scratchy hallucinations and all manner of phobias.

But mostly it was filled with rats. *Hundreds* of rats.

They crawled across the bar and up his hands and arms, before scurrying down his shaking legs. One tiny rodent nestled in his mohawk. His high-pitched scream was cut short as an imaginary rat ran into his mouth, its tail whipping his lips as it crawled ever deeper.

I bypassed the hallucinations and found his store of memories.

It didn't take much rifling to find what I was looking for. As soon as I had what I needed, I flitted back into myself and handed him a vial of coral-colored liquid. "Drink it, and it will all go away," I told him.

His hands trembled as he snatched the vial, and by the time his rats had faded to ghosts, I was gone.

-TWENTY ONE-

The supply room behind the bar was small, grungy and unremarkable, its shelves packed with brown and green glass bottles and its floor stacked with stainless steel kegs. One wall was empty but for boxes and a couple of old torn liquor posters affixed with duct tape.

It didn't take a wizard to spot the entire wall was an illusion. A slight shimmer ran over the brickwork and an eerie voice whispered in my mind, urging me to turn back.

Instead I walked through the wall. It felt like passing through a patch of freezing fog.

A bare bulb illuminated a flight of stone steps that led down into darkness. I trod lightly as a rumbling voice boomed in the distance and someone answered it in a bored, waspish tone.

The room below was huge; a warehouse of sorts, the walls and ceiling hewn from thick planks of oak. Most of the floor space was filled with tall racks loaded to the rafters with what I assumed were purloined goods. There were potions, glass cases full of snakes, bottles of glowing flies, bags of spices, and all manner of weapons. I walked carefully, to avoid the glow of the flickering lanterns mounted high upon the wooden walls, and did my best to ignore the allure of chests full of glimmering opals and thick bars of gold.

The entire place was how I'd imagined a pirate ship might look. And if the rumors were true, it quite possibly was exactly that, or at least in part.

I slunk along an aisle and paused when I spotted a figure curled up on a green velvet Victorian sofa. He wore a long black frock coat that made him look like a slightly irritable comma. The captain of the ship presumably. Argyle Screed.

He was thin with a mop of untamed pepper-colored hair and narrow blue eyes that glinted behind tortoiseshell glasses. He held a glass of red wine in one hand, and the other was placed against his forehead, as if he was suffering from some trying drama.

And then I saw the source of his irritation; a goliath with a bushy dark beard that spilled over his blood-spattered tunic and ended in a twist over his candy-striped trousers. It seemed like he was attempting, and failing, to count the stacks of money piled on the table before him. Both looked my way as I stepped into the light and the giant grunted as his hands turned to fists.

"And you are?" Argyle Screed enquired. He looked me up and down, before returning to his wine.

"Morgan Rook."

"You said it like it should mean something to me." Screed shrugged and took a full sip of wine. The goliath at the table began to stand.

I held a hand out. "I'm not here for trouble."

"And yet you've walked right into it." Screed set his glass down and held his hand over his eyes.

"What are you doing?" I asked. The floorboards shook and rumbled as the goliath bore down on me.

"Covering my eyes so I don't have to see you being squished. I cannot abide the sight of blood or squishing." Screed said. "Be fleet of fist Crispig, reintroduce Mr. Rook to the wall he mistakenly traversed."

Crispig, grabbed a scimitar from a shelf, charged and swung it. I ducked away. He was huge, a giant. His beard seemed to be part lichen and it was filled with tiny bone-colored creatures that twitched and scuttled within its strands.

"Get the hell away from me!" I growled. I didn't want to use my gun, not if I didn't have to.

If he heard me, he showed no sign of it. Instead he swung the blade, this time almost taking off the top of my head. The scimitar clanked against the wall, sending a shower of blue sparks flashing into the gloom.

I waited for him to strike again, then danced aside as the sword bit into the floorboards. I kicked the flat of the blade and sent it flying from his sweaty grasp.

Crispig swung his fist. It thundered into the side of my face and propelled me into a row of shelves. The world turned black but for a white hot spark that brought a roar of pain through my temples.

Another punch like that and I'd be out cold.

At best.

The goliath leaned down, his rancid beard in my face, the creatures inside scuttling madly. I pulled a lighter from my pocket, flipped it open and thumbed the flint wheel.

Crispig looked down as if this was some sort of joke. Then the tiny flames leaping across his beard, spread and began to singe and burn. Tiny skeletal creatures dropped from the fiery tangled mass and scuttled across the floor. Crispig howled as he fought to put the flames out but the fanning effect of his great hands causing them to spread even faster.

I grabbed what looked like a broken oar from a shelf, and smacked him hard across the head. There was a heavy *thunk* followed by an even heavier thud as he toppled onto the floor, out cold.

Clouds of dust rose around him as I stamped the flames out, my boot crunching the tiny white creatures like seashells.

A slow clap filled the room. "Bravo." Argyle Screed called. "Bravo indeed. But I wouldn't want to be you when he wakes. Crispig values his beard more than gold, which makes him a very cheap employee indeed."

"I'm here for information." I took some pleasure in the way Screed flinched as I strode towards him.

He raised a thin, arched eyebrow. "And why would I give you anything? You're an unwelcome guest. Like a tick, or a head louse."

"You know who I am, right?" I asked.

"I may be past my prime, but I'm not senile. You said your name was Morgan Rook, and I've no reason to doubt it." Screed pursed his wine stained lips. "I've heard of you. You're a bore who works for those even bigger bores at the Organization. A pimple on the side of an ass."

The man was ridiculous, but I admired his bravado. I swept my hand toward the shelves surrounding us. "The Organization takes a dim view of smugglers and magical contraband."

"And I take a dim view of the Organization." Screed's lips curled into a half smile. "And round and round it goes."

"Until one of us breaks, and I don't mean to be unkind, but I think we both know which of us is going to come off worse."

"Morgan Rook, scourge of vampires, ogres, and bearded bounders. It has a ring to it."

"It does. Now, let's stop trading insults and get down to business."

"Well the time for niceties is over," Screed said. "So what exactly is this information you seek?"

"I'm looking for a mercenary you employed."

Argyle Screed laughed. "I have nothing but mercenaries working for me, which is just how I like it. They're motivated by something that I have lots of and they don't demand health insurance. And come to think of it, most of the ones I hire can barely talk, and that's a definite bonus. Over the years I've employed countless meatheads, so you'll have to be a little more descriptive."

"A woman." I pulled my phone from my pocket and showed him a picture of the symbol. "She had a mark like this on her arm."

Argyle Screed nodded. "I remember her. She was good, but pricey. As I recall, she accompanied me on a jaunt overseas to pick up some most rare and precious...things."

"What's her name?"

"Hellwyn."

"Hellwyn what?"

"I've no idea of her surname, or if she even possessed one. In fact I cannot say I know much about her at all. She was most enigmatic and about as communicative as our formerly bearded friend sprawled out across my floor there."

I glanced at Crispig. Thankfully he was still out cold. "Where can I find her?"

"I don't know." Argyle Screed held his hands up as I advanced upon him. "All I know is if you require her service, you have to summon her."

"Summon her?"

"Yes. Or so I'm told. I didn't recruit her, I left that to a former associate."

"Former?"

"He came to a rather bloody end at the hands of a yeti."

"A yeti?"

Screed nodded, and by the displeasure on his face it seemed he was telling the truth. "Such a dreadful turn of events. Anyway the means of summoning Hellwyn died upon his half chewed lips. Which is a shame because she was most effective."

"That's not all you know." I could see he was holding something back, either to toy with me or to buy time for his goliath of a mercenary to wake up.

"The only other detail I can recall is my colleague mentioning something about finding her in a graveyard."

"Which graveyard?"

"I don't know, it was somewhere in the city. He said something about lighting a stump of candle clutched in the hands of a stone angel. All very gothic and mysterious, and utterly tiresome."

"Are you serious?"

"Deadly, and-"

Both of us glanced over as Crispig growled and began to raise his hand. It fell back down and landed with a great slap on the side of his face.

"You're welcome to join me for a glass of wine if you like," Argyle offered. "But if I were you, I'd take my leave. As I said, Crispig only has one joy in his rather limited life, and you set fire to it."

The giant groaned and his eyes opened wide. They fixed upon the ceiling, and then dropped to find me. He snarled.

I didn't like my chances of winning another round.

"Good evening, Morgan Rook," Screed called out as I turned and made my way down the aisles of contraband. "I trust I'll see you around."

"Count on it," I called back. "And if this information doesn't hold up, I'll do more than burn your idiot's beard."

"Most dramatic, Mr. Rook," Screed called. "Most dramatic indeed!"

I let him have the final word.

For now at least.

-TWENTY TWO-

I left The Seventh Knot and walked along the waterfront. The early evening air was cool and brought an autumnal breeze that rippled the water's muddy grey surface. The seasons were changing, and the idea of shorter days and long dark nights wasn't a welcome one.

Not with the way things were going in the city.

Every winter seemed to stir up new and terrible creatures. Coaxed by the darkness, they arrived eager to spill blood and feed before the bright scourge of summer drove a good number of them back into the shadows. Winter was high season for vampires, shadow kin and creeping death. And this year felt like it might be the most brutal yet.

I needed to find the assassin, before all hell broke loose. Once Tom was avenged, I could turn my attention back to Elsbeth Wyght. Then, and only then, could I even consider taking time off or hopping on a plane to sunnier climes.

My next step was to track down the mercenary. It was a loose, frayed thread, but it was the only thread I had. My phone screen glowed blue and bright in the gathering murk as I flicked through a list of the city's cemeteries.

There were more than I would have thought. Among the ones listed, I noted several names missing. So, clearly there'd be other long lost and forgotten ones that had managed to stay beyond the glare of the Internet's all-seeing eye. The thought of having to visit each of them looking for this stone angel was daunting. But if that's what it would take then so be it.

I had my gun and a few tricks in my bag, so at least I was ready. Graveyards weren't the best places to be after nightfall and were often magnets for all sorts of supernatural undesirables, ghouls, demons and...

Ghouls.

I'd encountered plenty of the creatures, but the word still conjured one particular image in my mind; Dauple. Dauple, the oddball. Dauple the Organization's chief collector of rare and exotic corpses. Dauple the ghoul.

Our last conversation, which had taken place over Tudor's partially dismembered corpse, returned to me. Specifically Dauple stating he'd been tailing the Organization's agents; the movers and shakers, and the *friends of crows*.

Surely if there was anyone who'd know every graveyard in the city, it was Dauple.

He was the best lead I had.

He was the only lead I had.

I dialed his number. It rang and rang. I hung up and tried again. Same thing.

Maybe he was asleep. After all, there was still a little daylight left in the corner of the sky. I pictured Dauple snoozing in a casket in some dimly lit cellar as he waited for night to set in.

I tried his phone again and hung up. I'd have to go and see him. The only problem being I only had the roughest idea of where he lived. He'd mentioned an apartment on the west side of the city and had hinted, unsubtly, that I should go and visit him. Hang out, drink whiskey, and talk about corpses, putrefaction or whatever the hell people like Dauple talked about in their downtime.

The wind blew with a bite of frost.

Perfect weather for hunting ghouls.

. . .

The neighborhood where Dauple lived suited him well, it was gloomy and shabby, its houses and buildings tall, narrow and neglected.

I got off the bus and wandered down the filthy sidewalk, spotted over the decades with old gum.

Where to go first? Dauple's breath was almost always laced with booze, so I expected he was more than a little familiar with the local dives.

I walked along a block riddled with pawn shops and thrift stores, past a takeout place. The window was filled with sweating columns of rancid looking meat turning on poles and just around the corner, an alley. I stopped.

Two tiny figures sat perched atop a trashcan sharing what looked like a bottle wrapped in a brown paper bag. At first I thought they were alcoholic children, and then I spotted the edge of the cloaks they were using to shield themselves from humans.

They were imps, their faces long, purple and pinched, their rheumy eyes mean-spirited. One wore a crumpled woolen hat, the other a hoodie.

I started towards them.

"Get out of here," the hatted one growled. It puffed out its chest and slicked its thin lips with an even thinner yellow tongue. "This is our alley."

"And you're welcome to it," I said. It was hard to tell if the creature was male or female below all the layers of clothes.

"He's still coming," the other said, punctuating each word with a belch. "But he shouldn't. Not if he knows what's good for him."

I could smell the booze now, an acrid stench of spoiled fruit and sugar. I could also sense their rising anger. Imps were treated pretty badly in the magical world, hence the colossal chips on their diminutive shoulders.

"Look." I tried to keep my voice friendly, "I just want some information."

"We're not leprechaunsss," one slurred. "If we knew where the friggin' pot of gold was we wouldn't be sitting on these trash cans getting rat-assed, would we?"

"Rat assed." The other nodded. "Plenty of rat asses 'round here. Especially down this alley. Is that what you're here for?" He glared at me. "You look like the kind of man who inspects rats' asses."

They laughed and the hatted one nudged the other with such force he almost fell off the trashcan. He grabbed the side of the lid to steady himself and as he did, he let go of the bottle.

His eyes widened in horror as it fell, hit the ground and shattered inside the bag. "Now look what you've done!" He howled, before fixing his blaming baleful eyes on me.

"Listen." I pulled some cash from my wallet. "I'll give you twenty bucks if you tell me what I need to know. That'll buy you a good three or four bottles of that rotgut."

They glanced at one other, whispered and conferred, then the hatted one turned back to me. "Two thousand dollars, and not a bean less." He dug his elbow into the other's ribs. "No, I meant three thousand. No, four. Yes, right?"

"That's a big ask seeing as you don't know what I want," I pointed out.

"Well we'd know if you friggin' well told us, wouldn't we?"

"I'm looking for a man named Dauple," I asked.

I could tell from the looks of disgust and repulsion in their eyes that they knew exactly who Dauple was.

"Urgh." They shook their heads in unison. "Him."

"Creepy bastard. Looks like a bony old goat," one slurred.

"No, he looks like a stork. A stork that stumbled through a Goth's wardrobe." the other added.

"That's definitely Dauple." I held out the twenty. "Where can I find him?" I snatched it away as one of them leaned over and tried to grab it.

"Five hundred and we'll tell you everything there is to know. Everything!"

I sighed. This was getting old and the sky was getting darker. "I'll give you thirty right now if you tell me where I can find him."

"Done!" The imp flexed his fingers.

I handed him the money. He snatched it away and leant over to kiss the notes with such enthusiasm that he fell off the can and landed on the ground in a crumpled heap. I reminded him of the question as I pulled him up to his feet.

He pointed to the other end of the alley. "Follow it round the bend. It comes out onto Dauple's street. Creepy sack of shit."

I wasn't sure if he was referring to Dauple or me. "What number?"

"I don't know nothing about numbers. I hate 'em. Never trust em'. Tricksy bastards."

The other glanced my way. "Look for his car," he said. "It's as long as winter and as black as a human heart."

"The hearse," I nodded.

"Oh, look at the Professor of words, hearse." The imp kicked the trashcan with the back of his heels. "You highfalutin bastard. I call it what it is, a shitmobile corpsecar!"

"Thanks." I walked away, choosing to ignore the long line of garbled insults that echoed along the alley behind me.

. . .

It didn't take long to spot Dauple's *shitmobile.* It was parked in front of a tall, ramshackle Victorian house that seemed about ready to collapse in on itself. The place looked like it had been subdivided into apartments and it didn't take Sherlock Holmes to figure out Dauple was in the basement.

Torn black sheets covered the windows and a heap of bulging trash bags were piled by the front door. A couple of them had split open, the spilled contents mostly consisted of empty wine bottles, oily red and white striped boxes and chicken bones.

A rancid smell of grease and decay filled the air, and flies buzzed all around.

I stepped gingerly down a short flight of cracked and shifting cement steps. I've fought vampires, trolls and ghasts, but Dauple's steps, they were an out and out deathtrap.

Light flickered in the large window and I caught sight of Dauple's chalky gaunt face.

I stood at the front door, its faded blue paint peeled and flaking. The thought of touching it was too disconcerting, so I delivered a sharp kick to its base instead.

Finally it opened.

"Morgan Rook!" Dauple grinned, revealing yellow and black teeth spotted with something gelatinous and blue. As if he'd been sipping ink, a possibility that wasn't entirely out of the question.

"Dauple." I nodded. "Look, I-"

"Come in." Dauple's bony fingers encircled my wrist and a heavy, sinking feeling passed through me as I was yanked into his dimly lit home. The buzzing drone of flies was even louder inside, his carpet was the color of moss and the wallpaper was bubbled, peeling and torn.

"This way. This way!" Dauple ushered me into a tiny living room. His sofa rested lopsidedly against one wall and for some reason, it had a large black hole scorched in the center of it. On one side was a wonky cabinet and a dusty vintage radio playing synth music from the eighties and a three-legged table that leaned against the arm of the sofa, supporting the remains of a Chinese takeout meal, as well as a syringe, which appeared to be filled with buzzing flies.

Dauple grabbed it and stuffed it under the blackened cushion. "Sit," he said.

"No, I-"

"Coffee? Rum? Chocolate milky? Haven't had a visitor in..."

Decades?

His eyes were glazed as he stumbled through to a small kitchen with an ancient old stove and a big pot full of something that smelled like dust, graves and last October's rain.

I sidled back to the living room, which seemed a fitting description, because who knew how many cultures of bacteria lived here.

Dauple returned moments later, bearing a dented platter, a chipped tea pot and a pair of styrofoam cups from a fast food joint. He poured thin amber liquid into the cup, and held it out with a shaking hand. "Drink," he said, with another toothy grin.

I mimed drinking the substance, which I hoped was whiskey, and watched as Dauple sipped from his own cup, his little finger extended in a strangely dainty fashion. "I'd have tidied up if I'd known..." Dauple's eyes drifted and then narrowed. "How'd you find me?"

"Imps."

"The alley lurkers? I've had more than my fair share of problems with those little shits. You wouldn't believe how many times I've reported them to the Organization, but-"

"Imps aren't exactly the Organization's highest priority. Look, I appreciate your hospitality, but I'm in a rush."

"How can I help you?" Dauple gave me an earnest look, eager as ever to impress. I knew he'd have given almost anything to be in my line of work, but the Organization had relegated him to an even lower rung then myself; corpse collector. "Do you know any graveyards-"

"I know every inch of every graveyard in this city. Every single one."

"I figured as much. I'm looking for one with a statue that holds a candle and-"

"Oh," Dauple said. "You're looking for *her*."

"The mercenary? You know her?"

"I know *of* her, and I know she's not someone to be trifled with."

"I don't want to trifle with her, I just want to talk to her."

Dauple set his cup down and led me from the room. "Come this way, I'll drive you to the graveyard. But I'm not hanging around there, not for anything."

I didn't think to ask why; I was more preoccupied with the thought of going anywhere in his hearse. But needs must when the devil drives. So I followed him from his rancid apartment as night sank its claws into the city.

-TWENTY THREE-

The graveyard was a square of wild green foliage fenced in by iron railings and surrounded by townhouses that had seen better days. The seatbelt felt damp and clammy as I unbuckled it and fought my way out of Dauple's hearse, anxious to escape reeked of death, decay and Dauple's boozy sweat.

"The statue you seek is in the dead center of the graveyard." Dauple's eyes flitted to my bag. "You're armed, yes?"

"Yeah. Why? What should I expect?" I glanced at the heavy brambles spilling over the rails. The graveyard's domestic surroundings hardly made it look like much of a threat, but looks could be deceiving.

"Who knows!" Dauple's eyes widened as he gazed through his filthy windscreen. "But the last time I was here I felt something watching me. It sent a cold shiver down my spine. I left immediately, didn't even finish cataloging the graves into my logbook."

A Logbook of graves...I didn't have the time or self-possession to ask so I thanked him for the ride, and left him to an evening of fun with his pet flies. He drove off in a cloud of exhaust, the car rattled around the block and vanished into the night.

I glanced around at the houses, most were dark but there were a few dimly lit windows that overlooked the graveyard. If the mercenary was keeping watch, she might well have lived in any one of them. Providing that was how she saw the signal. It was also possible she'd rigged magical elements that would alert her to the candle being lit, but spells could be traced and it seemed like privacy was high on her list of priorities. Plus, when it came to magic there were always costs, and most mercenaries I'd met were beyond tight.

I pushed the rusted gate open and entered the graveyard. It was a mess of tall wild grasses, overgrown shrubs and chipped, crumbling gravestones that leaned against one another in the moonlight.

The silence seemed to thicken as I made way toward the center, as if I were somehow miles away from the city. I passed a row of looming mausoleums and wandered through avenues of twisted trees, overgrown paths and broken railings.

Finally I found the stone angel, once white, now it was stained green with algae. Its wings were spread wide, its cupped hands held out. And there was the candle cradled in its palms.

I looked around, noting the houses with a clear line of sight through the vegetation, pulled my lighter out, flipped it open and sparked it into life. The candle sputtered as I lit the short damp wick and within moments the stump of wax glowed red and bright.

Wind stirred the leaves. I glanced around, expecting to find the mercenary standing in the shadows, but the graveyard was empty. Or appeared to be.

I waited a few moments and watched the windows, but there was nothing. So I blew out the candle and headed back through the graveyard, shivering as the air shifted and something scampered through the heavy brush.

It didn't take long to walk around the square. The houses were dull and unexceptional, but I caught a glimmer in a narrow alley between two buildings. It was a faint, colorful light, like the rainbow sheen of oil upon a puddle.

More of the light twinkled across the small garden in front of one particular house. Minor traps - nothing deadly, just simple deterrents for uninvited guests.

The doorbell was stiff and rigid, probably from lack of use. I pressed it hard, setting off a series of electronic chimes that rang deep within the house.

I peered through the small pane of glass in the door just in time to see a flicker of light at the top of a carpeted flight of stairs. It vanished as quickly as it had appeared, plunging the house into shadows.

If there was anyone home, they certainly didn't want to be seen.

I ran my hand across the doorknob but drew it away as a heavy cold sensation passed through my fingers and seeped into my bones. The lock was enchanted. Using magic to break it would take more effort than I could spare. Luckily I had another trick in my bag, a ring of skeleton keys. Eventually I found one that fit.

Thankfully the dead bolts weren't drawn, but as I pushed the door it gave a loud moaning creak. "Shit."

So much for stealth.

The house was silent but for the tick of a distant clock and the heavy drip of a tap. I grasped a crystal, closed my eyes, and absorbed it along with some of the magic thrumming through the walls and ceilings. I focused my thoughts and let it wash over me until I was fully charged and ready to go.

The first room I searched was a sparse, vacant living room; the kitchen was empty too.

I made my way up the stairs, my heart pounding as I unclipped my holster.

Something was off about this place, but I couldn't put my finger on it.

The upstairs was as silent and still as the ground floor. I checked a bedroom, and a large spotless bathroom and found nothing.

One room to go.

I pushed the door open and slipped into a second moderately sized bedroom. It was furnished with thick heavy curtains, a queen-sized bed, a wardrobe and a tall freestanding mirror. The room appeared to be empty, but someone was watching. I could feel it. I scanned for the blink of a camera and checked the walls for tell-tale signs of magically cloaked figures. There was nothing. The mirror caught my eye as I crept past it, My reflection had moved a little too slowly, like it was a split second behind.

"There." I reached into my bag and pulled out an iron wand and ran it across the mirror's surface. It flickered with blue swirls of light. An enchantment.

I was about to counteract the spell when the door downstairs creaked open.

-TWENTY FOUR-

I gripped the handle of my gun. Moonlight filtered through the windows, illuminating the top of the staircase as a silhouette passed. The light was too dim to see in detail, it was just a dark form but I could tell it was hooded.

The assassin?

My heart raced as I considered the killer's murderous efficiency and its seemingly limitless threshold for pain.

Could a bullet stop it?

I placed a foot out to steady myself. As I brought my gun up and took aim, the fleeting memory of Tom's last moments flashed through my mind.

I saw him falling dead in the dirt.

I saw his eyes being scooped from his face.

Come on you bastard.

A door creaked along the hall.

It was searching the house, just as I had. This room was next, I had seconds left.

I decided to meet it head on. I was about to inch towards the landing when someone grabbed me from behind and yanked me back.

I fell, tumbling into what could only be the mirror. The glass was icy cold and swelled around me like water. Like plunging into the wintry Pacific surf at dawn.

There was no crash, no chime, no tinkle of broken glass.

There was no sound at all.

Just silence and darkness.

-TWENTY FIVE-

The arm clamped around my neck and held me like a vise. I still had my gun in hand and considered firing blindly behind me, until a woman whispered, "Not a word. Or we both die."

Several words came to mind, none of them good, so I forced myself to swallow them and gave a slight nod. She had the advantage.

For now at least.

I stared back through the mirror, it was like a thick sheet of ice. Cold darkness pressed around the portal and I could hear a distant sound of rushing air.

The view of the bedroom through the glass was a back-to-front glimpse of the world I'd just left behind. I was somewhere else.

But where?

The Hinterlands? That fabled realm between realms?

My racing thoughts ceased as a shadow fell over the glass and crept across the patch of carpet before the opening. The assassin stepped into view, a short sword clenched in its gloved hand.

Its movements were silent, all I could hear were the controlled shallow breaths from the woman behind me. We watched as the assassin searched the room, then it turned to face the mirror and leaned in close, its dead, soulless eyes piercing through the glass.

Terror and rage flooded through me. I tried to raise the gun to blow the bastard's head off.

"I told you not to move," the woman whispered.

I grabbed her hand and twisted. She released me. "Idiot," she growled.

I paid her no mind. The assassin's eyes narrowed, it cocked its head. It had heard us.

It reached towards the glass.

I took aim.

"I really wouldn't do that." The woman's voice was receding, her footfall drawing away. The assassin tapped a finger upon the glass, the sound was like cannon fire.

I cocked the hammer as it drew back its fist to strike the glass.

I fired.

Light exploded through the murk and the roar of the gun was like a blow to the head.

The world shook, the mirror splintered, then everything went black.

-TWENTY SIX-

Was I dead? Had the journey into the Hinterlands wrenched my soul from my body?

It took a moment to put the pieces together but the fact that I was still thinking meant I was most likely still alive. This realization was confirmed as I felt every single ache and bruise in my body.

"Hello?" I called.

Someone moved in the darkness, a reddish black silhouette stepping away through the swirling gloom. A bitter laugh receded into the distance, followed by what sounded very much like *fucking idiot.*

I ran until the footfalls ahead came to a stop.

"What part of *not a word or we both die* did you not understand?" A flame sparked to life, illuminating the woman holding it.

She was shorter than me, but only just, and older too. Fury glinted in her iron-grey eyes and flashed like lightning as she glared at me. Her silver streaked raven black hair was pulled back into a pony-tail and her mouth was drawn into a well-used, mocking smile.

She wore a simple fitted coat and trousers that seemed to be made from battered black leather, and a glimmer of light ran through them. It was the same glimmer I'd noticed on Tom's raincoat when the attacker had struck. "Where are we?" I glanced into the darkness around us.

"Where do you think we are?"

"The Hinterlands...the in-between?"

"Bingo!" The woman dropped the match, plunging us into darkness.

The blinding gloom was overwhelming and disconcerting, then a beam of light appeared on the hard stone ground. It caught the sheathed sword by the woman's side. "Are you Hellwyn?" I asked.

She gazed at me for a moment, and gave a slight nod. "I am. And if you don't tell me who you are, and what the hell you were doing in my house, I'll leave you to the darkness." Her smile was hard and tight. "I'd give you five minutes of survival at best."

"I'm Morgan Rook."

"Really." She gave me a long, frosty look. "And you were prowling around in my house, because?"

"Because I was looking for you."

"Yes, I saw you in the graveyard."

"Why didn't you come?"

"I didn't like the look of you, and I still don't. Who sent you?"

"No one."

"Really? You're not from the Organization?"

It was amazing how much scorn she managed to inject into that single word. I decided to try another tack. "I came to help you."

She snorted. "Help me? How?"

"The man trying to kill you-"

"It's not a man."

"Then what is it?"

"Carry on. You were about to explain how you think you can help me."

"Look, that thing...whatever it is....it killed my friend, Tom."

Her sneer melted. "Tom was a good man." She sighed. "And a fool. I can't believe he's gone. He should have retired years ago. I told him. Quit, spend your last few years propping up bars in some faraway place. Eat, drink, be merry. Go to ground. That's what I told him. But instead he stayed on the streets."

"How -"

A thud came from somewhere in the darkness.

Hellwyn's fingers closed around the pommel of her sword. "That's a creature looking for a way in, and it may find one." She strode off, her flashlight playing across the cavern-like floor. I dug around in my pocket for my phone. I wanted my own light. I looked up as I heard her stop.

"Are you coming, Morgan Rook, or do you want to stay here in the dark? I'd advise against it. Things lurk in these shadows...and they're not very nice." She strode away. I ran to catch up.

We walked in silence, our footsteps punctuated by depth-charge like thuds that seemed to echo all around us in the gloom. It was difficult to get a clear picture of where we were, but it sounded, by the echo of our boots, like we were in a tunnel and far off in the distance was a flickering light. I reached out, searching for a wall, and recoiled as an icy-cold wetness brushed against my fingers.

"I wouldn't do that," Hellwyn said, as she continued at a pace. "Reach out into the darkness and it just might reach back. It's how things are here."

"I still don't understand where *here* is." Naturally I'd heard the rumors and tales of the otherworld, and the spaces in-between, but it wasn't a subject I'd really been drawn to. I already had more than enough problems dealing with one reality, let alone worrying about others.

"Think of this place as a crawlspace between worlds. The true middle of nowhere, the place the forgotten things go." Hellwyn trained her flashlight upon a wall. It was made of rugged black rock. "Or perhaps, the things best forgotten."

Her light passed over an opening that looked like a huge glass porthole thick with algae and mold. I leaned towards it and recoiled as a giant face gazed back at me. It was huge and pale, its flesh the color of a fish's belly. Two great pits, just above its cavernous mouth, formed its eyes.

As I looked into those deep empty spaces, I felt a terrible urge to smash my fists against the glass, to help the watcher through.

It reached towards me, its fingers unfurling like a sea anemone. They drummed on the porthole, producing the deep, booming sound once more. The din passed through the glass, through my fingers and into the very center of my mind.

Strange noises swirled all around me, eerie deformed sounds like whales in the deep, their calls slow and warped. But there was another layer to it. At first it seemed like tv static, then like matches being struck. *Thousands* of matches. I suddenly realized they were voices, each imploring me to smash the glass and let the creature through.

"I will!" I heard myself call. I had to shatter the barrier, to free the giant from its prison. I drew back my fist to pummel the glass, when someone grabbed my wrist and yanked me away.

Hellwyn spun me around and shone her light deep into my eyes, then she slapped me hard and fast.

The sound of static left my mind and I found myself back in the here and now.

"Maybe you'll stick to the path now? Like I told you to. Yes?"

I nodded, trying not to glance back towards the porthole. I had no idea what the being behind the glass had intended, but it definitely felt malevolent and I was certain it had almost fractured my mind.

I shrugged, determined not to show my distress, but Hellwyn's mocking grin said she'd seen it well enough.

A blast of cold air whistled along the tunnel and I caught the scent of wood smoke. Flickering fires gleamed in the distance and every now and then silhouetted figures flitted in front of them.

"Who are they?"

Hellwyn ignored my question, pulled a round silver object from her pocket and flipped it open. It looked like some kind of compass, its needle glowing radioactive green. I stumbled along behind her as she walked. Then she stopped and flashed her light across the floor. Faint chalk-like markings covered a section of stone, strange symbols that seemed to be drawn from some alien alphabet.

I took a step back as Hellwyn reached up and placed her hand against my forehead. My skin tingled, it felt like something had passed between us, some kind of unseen spell. "What was that?" I asked.

"Permission for you to follow. An arcane guest pass if you will. Now let's go, and don't tarry." Hellwyn reached toward the shadows and nodded to me as she stepped into the darkness. It swallowed her whole.

I froze, my heart pounding hard, then I gazed down the long black corridor to the flickering light from the distant bonfires. Another figure flitted by, it was tall, crane-like but almost human in form with a narrow, elongated head and a full distended belly. The sight of it filled me with dread and indecision.

"Rook!"

I flinched as a hand reached from the shadows, grabbed my wrist and pulled me into the darkness.

-TWENTY SEVEN-

I found myself in a small room lit by a hanging lantern and a couple of oil lamps resting on top of an old crate. The walls were rough pitted stone and the place was barely warmer than the drafty passage beyond.

A makeshift camp bed rested alongside a rickety wooden chair. The opposite wall was obscured by a large wardrobe and in the middle of the floor in front of it sat an oversized wooden chest, the kind you'd see in a pirate movie. I wondered if it had once belonged to Argyle Screed.

I caught a flash of steel as Hellwyn opened the wardrobe. One side was taken up with weapons. Swords, daggers and lethal-looking implements I couldn't name. The other side was filled with simple black garments.

Hellwyn swapped the sword from her belt for a new weapon. Light shimmered across the new blade and vanished as she slid it into her sheath.

"I've got a spare gun," I offered. "If you fancy joining me in the twenty-first century."

"A gun is next to useless in the Hinterlands. You'll need silver, steel or iron, especially when it's time to get up close."

I reached into my shoulder bag. "I've got other stuff besides guns."

Hellwyn ignored me and pulled a bottle of gin from the wardrobe, along with a battered tin cup. She splashed out a large measure, closed her eyes and drank it down. Then she poured another shot and offered it to me. "It will ground you."

It was dry and had a sharp aftertaste that lingered after the burn that scorched its way down my throat. Gin wasn't my drink at the best of times, but this stuff was particularly vile. "What's in it? That wasn't straight booze."

"Essence of hazeldim, a berry that grows in the wilds here. That's the part that'll help ground you...gin just gets you drunk, but it's the best way to make the infusion." Hellwyn grabbed the cup from me, filled it, and took another hefty sip.

A warm buzz clouded my head, it was almost enough to take the edge off the recent events. I sat on the chair and leaned back, enjoying the rush of blood to my head. "You said the assassin isn't a man. So what is it?"

"Unexpected." Hellwyn's eyes darted over me in a strange, appraising way. She looked like she was trying to reach a decision, and then she gave a low, resigned sigh. "It's called a Hexling. Think of it as a golem, but faster and fleeter. I haven't seen one in...in a very long time."

"Why's it after you?"

"I don't know." The ice in her eyes melted. Just a little. "Someone's sent it to murder me, just like Tom and the others."

"Others?"

The steel returned to her voice. "Don't take me for a fool. You know about the other victims, and I know more about you than you realize."

"Like what?"

"Like the fact that you're a one-eyed man in the kingdom of the blind. A man who earns his pennies working for a hidden outfit that serves ruthlessly ambitious bureaucrats."

"Look-"

"Are you denying it?"

"There's worse things to be paid for than taking out dangerous shitheels. Or would you prefer having rogue vampires running round the city feeding on people? Or shifters raping and pillaging? Or demons-"

"I don't deny the Organization has its time and place, just don't fool yourself when it comes to who's pulling the strings." Her eyes flitted over me again. "You're human, right?"

"As far as I know." It was a lame attempt at humor, but the truth was, some pretty odd memories had been resurfacing and I had no real certainty of what I was. Or where in the hell I belonged. "Look, I didn't come here for insults, I came to help."

"Help? In the same way you *helped* Tom? You have his blood on your hands."

My bewilderment turned to rage. "Why in the hell would you say that?"

"He told me about you." Hellwyn poured another generous measure of gin and drained it in a single gulp. "He spent years watching out for you, and he never stopped, not even after you were able to look after yourself. Tell me, did you ever think that maybe you should look out for him too?"

I remained silent and fought to control the anger blazing inside me.

Hellwyn opened the wooden chest, pulled something out and tossed it to me.

Tom's old raincoat. It smelled of age but it looked like it had been well kept. The cloth was clean and the cut was vintage; a well made garment from a bygone era. She reached back into the chest and threw a short, sheathed sword onto the bed beside me.

"How did you get them?"

"Tom and I had a bond. And even though I was far away I felt his distress in those final moments. His terror, his resignation, and the darkness surrounding him. Everything felt charged, like the air before a storm. By the time I got to him, it was too late. I took his effects and got out of there before the police arrived. He wanted you to have them. And now you do."

"I don't know why. I barely knew him."

Hellwyn's eyes misted over as she glanced at the coat. She wiped them, and they became as hard as flint once more. "Just put it on."

I did as she asked. The coat was long, its fabric thin, but somehow it felt solid. Strong almost. A faint shimmer ran across it and the cuffs began to shorten to fit my wrists. I looked down to see the coat's length adjust itself to reach just below my knees. "What is this thing?"

"Armor. It goes with the sword."

"Armor?"

Hellwyn pulled her sword from its scabbard and swung it towards me. I barely had time to flinch as it cleaved towards my chest. Sparks ran along the blade and it bounced off with a clang. As if the coat was made of stone.

"Like I said," Hellwyn lowered her sword. "Armor. The enchantment is very powerful. Not that it helped Tom. But nothing can save a man who believes his time has come."

"Why did he believe that?"

"Guilt." Hellwyn slopped more gin into her cup. She drank half and passed me the remainder.

The thought of drinking the muck wasn't a welcome one, but I forced it down. Its bite was no less strong the second time round.

"Guilt for what?"

"Something that happened a long time ago in a place far from here. Another time, another world." A bittersweet smile played across her lips. "He had nothing to be guilty for. We simply had a job to do and we did it. Tell me, do you ever feel a scrap of remorse for the lives you snuff out?"

"Now and then. But I have to remind myself of the people I'm protecting. Sometimes you have to take lives to save lives. "

Hellwyn nodded. "Sadly, Tom didn't see things that way." She tipped the bottle over the cup. A few drops splashed into the tin. "Damn it. Have you got anything worthwhile in that bag of yours?"

"Booze? No."

"Why am I not surprised? You're more of a hindrance than a help."

I'd had enough of the snide remarks. If she didn't want my help, why continue to hang around? This was a waste of precious time. I walked back to the wall and prepared to step through.

"Leaving?" Hellwyn asked.

"Clearly I'm not welcome here."

I reached for the wall but faltered as she spoke once more. This time there was a scrap of humility in her voice. "I'm sorry."

For a moment I caught a glimpse of the woman below the frosty exterior. Fierce pride still shone in her eyes, but it was softening now. I nodded. Holding a grudge seemed pretty foolish. "Don't worry about it."

"You really want to help?" This time there was no scorn in her voice.

"Yes. I want to see the murderous piece of shit who killed Tom dead."

"Then we'll have to work together. There are two enemies. The Hexling and whoever's controlling it."

"How do we find them?"

"I don't know. But there's still some of the Order left. At least I hope there is. Maybe someone will have an answer."

"What Order?"

Hellwyn shook her head. "It doesn't matter, not now. I'll tell you more when I'm certain you're capable of helping."

"Look, I don't have my resume handy, but-"

"Stop the flippancy, I need you to listen."

"I am listening."

"The Hexling isn't going to be like anything you've ever fought. Guns, magic tricks...they won't work against it, you need steel and cold purpose. Which is another reason I followed Tom's wishes and gave you his sword. It's sharp. Very sharp, but only if its wielder uses their full intent."

"I've got plenty of intent. Mostly revenge."

"Killing's not the only intent you'll need when you fight the Hexling. It's fast, fleet and utterly deadly. You'll need to parry, block and divert as well as strike." She touched the side of her head. "We have one thing it doesn't - minds of our own. And yours needs to be razor sharp."

"It's probably a good thing we ran out of gin then."

She almost smiled. "I suppose." Hellwyn lifted her sword and nodded for me to do the same. "Now block me."

She sprang forward, her sword flashing through the air. I pulled Tom's sword up to block it, and barely stopped her blade from slashing the side of my face.

Hellwyn lowered her sword. "I could have cleaved your head off if I'd intended to. Let's try again. This time focus, use your intention to stop my attack."

The sword flashed again as it swung towards me.

Stop.

My hand tingled as the blade came up to meet hers. I braced myself and allowed the energy flowing through the pommel to strengthen my resolve and block the attack. The blades clashed and I pushed her back.

"Better." Hellwyn lowered her blade. For a moment I thought it was over, then she swung again.

Her sword whistled through the air. I brought my own up.

Back.

The blades clashed with a scrape of steel and a charge of electric-blue light. I focused my strength, it ran through the blade and pushed her away, and then I twisted the blade, almost wrenching hers from her hand.

"You've done this before." She almost sounded impressed.

"No. Not that I recall."

"You might not consciously remember but you're definitely utilizing muscle memory. Maybe you'll survive this after all."

"You're filling me with confidence. So you think we'll be able to stop the assassin?"

"There's a chance."

"So, if we do, how will we find whoever's been controlling it?"

"I don't know," she said. But the look in her eyes said otherwise.

"You know more than you're telling me. I can't work blind, Hellwyn."

"I don't know anything, but I suspect plenty. Not that any of it makes much sense. But it bears all the hallmarks of someone we once dealt with..." Hellwyn shook her head, "but he's dead. *Long* dead."

"Who was he?"

"It's irrelevant. History. It belongs in the past."

"Not if it's affecting the present."

"It doesn't, it can't. It would be impossible. We'll find out more when we defeat the Hexling. Once it's down we'll examine it and hopefully find some indications of who's sent it."

"Right. Let's go then."

"No, not until I know you're strong enough to fight it. There's no way I'm going into combat with one arm tied behind my back."

I sighed. This was getting old. "So how are you going to know I'm worthy?"

A sinking feeling passed through me as her lips twisted into a semblance of a smile. "I'll know if you survive."

"Survive what?" The sinking feeling grew even heavier.

"You seem to think you're some sort of hero, Morgan Rook. So let's put you to the test."

"How?"

"By doing what all heroes do. By facing the beast."

-TWENTY EIGHT-

"What beast?" I asked, even though I wasn't sure I really wanted to know.

"This part of the Hinterlands is relatively safe, with the exception of the Gloaming Ghasts that lurk within the walls. But they're easily avoided...by anyone with half a brain, at least."

"You mean the giant creature at the window? You want me to go after it?" I didn't know how I was going to react if she said yes.

Thankfully, she shook her head. "It's tempting, but it wouldn't be a fair battle. No, I want you to fight a very different kind of beast. As I said, the Hinterlands are passages between worlds. Some use it like a corridor, they cross from one world to another. But others choose the Hinterlands as a destination, a sanctuary, a place to disappear off the grid so to speak."

"Like the people around the campfires?"

"No. And they're not people, you should stay away from them. You need to locate a human family. Once you find them, you'll find the beast. I'm certain of it."

"Are they humans from my world?"

Hellwyn gave me a curious look, and shook her head. "I don't think so. Actually, I have no idea where they came from, but there are five of them. Or there were. A father, a mother, and three toddlers. They entered the tunnels within the last week and that was the last anyone saw of them."

"Maybe they were looking for some quiet time."

"Well, if they were, they didn't find it. My associate told me he'd heard screams echoing up from the deep levels. Terrible cries of pain and suffering. I was called to investigate, but now that you're here...."

"What is this place?"

"A city whose name is long forgotten. Ruins for the most part. Beyond it are the Hinterlands proper, but you're not going there. You're headed down, into the deeps."

"Right." The sinking feeling in my stomach was stronger than ever, but I did my best not to show it. "So what kind of beast am I looking for? I need to know what I'm dealing with."

"I wish I could tell you, but no one who's seen it has lived to tell the tale."

This was getting better and better. I checked through my bag.

"You need to leave your bag here. And your gun."

"Are you serious?"

"Perfectly. This is your test."

"But-"

"Your bag's just full of props. You don't need them. Not like you think you do."

"I need the crystals. For magic. I'm not a natural like you."

"Do you trust me?" Hellwyn asked.

Hell no. But I knew she was my best hope for finding Tom's killer and the only hope for finding my way out of here. "I guess."

"You have armor," she waved a hand towards Tom's coat, "and your sword. Follow the passage toward the fires. There's a turn just before you reach the main chamber, take the stairs down to the lower levels. Simple. Now go and do what needs to be done."

"How do I find my way back? *If* I..."

"Take this." Hellwyn pulled a silver chain from around her neck. A charm hung from it, an arrowhead made of amber. Then she held out to her hand and showed me the amber ring on her index finger. "They were carved from the same stone and they're a pair, therefore they belong together." She handed me the necklace. "As soon as they're apart they'll start glowing, and they'll get dimmer and dimmer the further you go. Which means, on your way back, the closer you are the brighter it'll get."

"I should try to get something similar for my house keys."

"Do you always make lame jokes when you're scared?"

"Yeah, pretty much. Well, I'll see you soon then. Hopefully." I didn't wait for her response, I stepped through the wall and emerged into the darkness.

The only light came from the distant glimmer of the bonfires and the sudden glow of Hellwyn's pendant. I slipped it below my shirt and started down the tunnel, my attention focused on the figures in the chamber ahead.

My hand strayed toward the strap of my bag and closed on nothing. It was just me, a raincoat and an ancient sword.

A cold draft blew down the corridor and I walked quietly among the smell of damp and decay and edged towards the tunnel's end.

Thud.

The hair on the back of my neck prickled as I turned to find a porthole in the shadowy wall behind me. A huge pale face looked out. I glanced away from its gaze and hurried on, my skin crawling as I felt those cavernous eyes follow me.

Sounds drifted through the chamber, whispers, the crackle and spit of flames, and heavy footfalls. The figures huddled around the fires reminded me of the people in the homeless camp where I'd finally found Tom. But these weren't people. They were too tall, or too short, their heads long ovals, their eyes bright yellow flashes of light.

One of them froze and cocked its head, its eyes narrowing as it stared into the darkness toward me.

I remained still and waited until finally it turned its attention back to the fire.

As I inched closer to the chamber I spotted the passage Hellwyn had mentioned. I ducked into it, glad to be out of view of the twisted figures tending their fires.

The passage was pitch black. I pulled my phone from my pocket, glad Hellwyn had either missed it, or disregarded my taking it with me. It felt strange in my hand, utterly out of place in this otherworldly realm. The glow of the display was swallowed up by the unearthly darkness and did little to light my way, all I could see were thick stone walls and a flight of worn stairs leading down. I turned the flashlight app on, pointed the beam toward my feet and made my way down the steps.

I reached the bottom where a long corridor stretched out before me, its walls lit by eerie, pulsing, glowing blue and green lights. But as I reached them I saw they weren't lights, but some kind of fungus. It trembled and twitched as I leaned in to inspect it. It looked like bracket fungi; long shelf-like rows of fruiting mushrooms.

The place reeked of damp and mold and a cold draft issued along the corridor. I strode on but slowed as something moved in the darkness ahead.

I reached for my gun but it wasn't there. "Shit."

I pulled the sword from its sheath but it felt *wrong*. Like it was simply a costume prop, like I was eleven years old once more, playing pirates with my friends.

And then a white pinprick of light appeared in the gloom and I could see the outline of a person coming towards me.

I pocketed the phone and held the sword with both hands. Was this the beast?

No, it was a woman...

My gorge rose as she shuffled into the halo of light radiating from the fungus.

She wore a moth-eaten wool dress, caked in dirt, and blood.

Her lips were half chewed off, her face a map of festering wounds. One of her eyes was missing, the other the color of curdled milk. It glowed as it jiggled in its socket and fixed upon me.

She moaned and reached out with broken fingers, her other arm ending in little more than a stump encrusted with dry blood.

A zombie.

"Great." I held the sword out as she shambled forward, gnashing her chipped shards of teeth together. A stench of bile and rot leaked from her half open throat.

And then with a hoarse cry of rage, she lunged at me.

-TWENTY NINE-

I jumped aside as the zombie turned to strike again. She snapped and groaned. The stench of rot and decay was overwhelming. I wanted to run, put as much distance between myself and this abomination as possible but I knew she'd follow me. Besides, I never run, not when I can help it.

The zombie darted and pounced, her twisted clawed fingers jutting toward my face. I stepped back and allowed my thoughts to focus, to stream from my mind, through my limbs and into the sword.

She attacked again.

Cut.

The sword almost danced as I swung, it bit through her wrist and cleaved off her hand. It fell to the ground with a soft thump as she hissed and lumbered on.

End.

I swung the sword again. My focus on her throat, my intent to decapitate, to put an end to her monstrous wretched half life. The blade slipped through her flesh spilling blood as thick and sluggish as crude oil.

Her eye glowed with a piercing light and I'd swear I heard a strangled, half human plea. Then the crimson line across her throat yawned open and her head toppled to the ground, followed by her jittering, thrashing form.

I sheathed the sword, grabbed my phone and took off down the tunnel, eager to escape the sound of the twitching corpse behind me.

One tunnel led to another, twisting and turning, the grime and dirt growing thicker the further I went. Great tangled webs dangled over the path, I held my breath as I strained to listen for the approach of the unimaginable creature that must have woven them. More tunnels, more twists. Soon the glowing fungus grew in such proliferation that I no longer needed my phone to light the way.

Bones littered the floor. Nestled amongst them were skulls, some human, some canine, but most I could not identify. I paused to take a closer look and realized that many belonged to a species of large formidable looking beasts I'd never seen. Nor wanted to.

With the exception of my own footfalls, the place was silent. I tried to walk quietly but now and then the crunch of tiny shards of bones rang out, giving my position away to anything that might be lurking in this god forsaken place.

It seemed like I'd been wandering for hours in the still, abandoned depths when two new tunnels appeared. They branched off to my left and right while the tunnel I'd been following led to a shadowy flight of stairs that plunged into darkness. I paused as an eerie sound drifted up from below. A voice. It was too muffled to for me to understand the words, but it sounded like a man, his voice low and urgent, his cadence almost sing-song.

The hairs on the back of my neck prickled and once again I reached for my bag of tricks and gun. I felt so frigging naked without them, vulnerable.

Slowly, I made my way down the steps.

An empty doorway awash with firelight yawned at the foot of the stairs and the flickering light spread across the flagstoned floor. The splintered remains of two wooden doors hung from heavy black iron hinges and, through the large gaps and holes that had been punched through the wood, I could see a long open room. One wall was lit by flaming torches, while the other danced with shadows. In the center was a row of benches, like pews in a church.

Three small figures sat huddled at the front, their silhouettes leaning against one another as if drunk or asleep. They faced the man standing before them. His voice was louder now. "...the princess lived in a castle surrounded by gardens and sunlit dells, and trees laden with the plumpest, juiciest fruits you've ever seen."

I crept into the room and edged along the shadowy walls. If the man had seen me, he showed no sign of it, he just continued with his story.

There was madness in his voice. Madness and despair.

He wore what might once have been a nice coat, nut-brown with patched elbows, now ragged and torn. His hair was greasy and wild and hung in curtains, almost obscuring his round wire-framed glasses.

He looked like an accountant lost in the wilds of some terrible place.

A place just like this.

I glanced toward the three figures on the bench, I could not see their faces but I could tell they were children. They remained frozen as the man clawed his fingers and his raised voice boomed in the character of a fairy tale beast.

There's only one beast here. I had no idea where the thought came from, but I knew it was true. Then I noticed the string tied around the children's arms and legs, pulled taut to keep them sitting up and at attention. The chill running across the nape of my neck was consumed by a hot flash of rage.

"...and do you know what the princess was called?" the man continued, seemingly unaware of my presence. Light flickered upon his glasses as he cocked his head towards his audience.

I drew parallel with the children. A flood of bile rose, stopping just short of my mouth.

They were dead, their throats slashed, their garments spattered with blood. Each sweet tiny porcelain face was frozen with horror, their wide glassy eyes staring.

His captive audience.

-THIRTY-

"It's not how it seems." The man turned to me. "Now please, step out from the shadows and show yourself."

Rage simmered through me. "It's not how it seems? You mean those children aren't bound and their throats aren't slashed?" My fingers gripped the pommel of my sword.

"What are you doing here, in our home?" The man asked, his voice broken and insane. "It's far too late for visitors."

"I'm looking for a monster and I think I just found it."

"There's no monster here." He shook his head decisively. "Now, you must go. I need to finish the story before I put my children to bed." He pointed to a series of makeshift beds, each carefully covered with a thick blanket of dust and silken cobwebs.

"Why did you do it?" I asked. I could barely move or think as the utter horror washed over me in ever more powerful waves. "Why?"

He glanced back to his slain audience. "I...I had to save them."

"Save them. By cutting their throats?"

His brow furrowed. "Do you think it was an easy choice for a father to make?"

I pulled my sword from its sheath and held it by my side.

"You'll never understand what it was like,' he continued, one finger pointing my way, "never!"

"Tell me why." There was no question, I was going to kill him, but before I did I had to make sense of this evil.

"We came to escape." The man smiled, exposing small yellow teeth. "Go to the Hinterlands they said, you'll be safe there. What choice was there? We couldn't't stay where we were, the whole place teeming with them. People turning, transforming into those...into those things. I didn't want to watch my family suffer like that, and nor did I want to suffer that fate myself." He trailed off and gazed into the darkness behind me.

"What fate?"

"The sickness," he said. "The pestilence that turned the dead to living and the living to dead. We fled, left everything; our possessions, our gold, our home. As well as my research. All gone. We ventured through the forbidden caves and finally we were delivered to...safety." He gave a short, bitter laugh. "Tell me, does it seem like a safe place to you?"

I had no answer for him.

"I thought it could be a fresh start, or that we could at least ride it out. Hide for a while, gather our thoughts and wits, and once we had, find a new land. A place for the living. And we would have too, I believe that."

"What happened?"

"I thought we'd left the darkness behind, but we'd brought it along with us."

He stepped into the light of the flaming torch and now I could see his face more clearly, the tiny veins in his forehead inky blue and black, the yellow tinge of his eyes and his bloody gums as he smiled. "My wife had been bitten. She'd hidden it from me. Hid her shame and terror. Perhaps she thought the infection would simply vanish once we left our world. That's what I tell myself."

He stepped towards me. I clenched my sword tighter.

"She's wandering out there even now. Lost and alone." He nodded towards the door.

I thought of the woman in the wool spun dress and shivered. "What about the children?"

"I'd been out foraging. Some of the fungus in the tunnels is perfectly nutritious, and there's a cavern with a pool of water and fish. Revolting things, but edible. I was only gone for a few hours but when I came back..." He stopped, choked by his words. "When I came back she'd turned and.... bitten my little angels." He took a deep breath, his hands clenched to fists as he moved closer to me.

"And then what?" I took a step away. The wall was right at my back.

"She returned to her senses. For a few scant moments at least. I took her away, dragged her through the tunnels like a savage dog. I set her free at a crossroads and she wandered off. That was the last I saw of her."

I already knew the story's end, but he continued.

"And then I bound up my angels so they couldn't harm each other and I went in search of help. But there was none. This place is filled with hard, soulless creatures. Everyone's out for themselves. No one cares." He shook his head. "Maybe that's not true. Some did show mercy, but none could help. They thought I might find a cure, in some other world. So I came back to collect my angels...but they were lost, burning up, turning...I couldn't bear to watch. So I...so I ended their torment."

"I'm so sorry," I said as I sheathed the sword.

"Sorry?" He smiled. "It seems like such a tiny little word." He pointed to his forehead. "Can you see them, the black worms crawling through my veins?" The edge crept back into his voice.

"It looks like an infection."

"*The* infection. Soon I'll be one of...them," he nodded to the children. "Which is why I was set to spend one last night with my angels. But you arrived." He pointed to my sword. "You look like a man who's no stranger to violence and death. Help me end it."

"I don't understand," I said, even though I did.

"End my life, then burn this room to charcoal. Stop the sickness from spreading."

I was filled with apprehension. Killing him the moment I'd seen the children would have been one thing, but after he'd told me the truth? Now that I knew of the heartbreaking, hideous choice he'd had to make and how it had sent him over the edge?

He sniffed the air. "You carry so many scents. So many worlds. So much death. You've dealt more than your fair share of endings. All I'm asking for is one more. A mercy killing."

"I can't. It's not how I do things. There has to be a reason-"

"Is this not reason enough?" He cried. The black worms in his forehead began to squirm.

"This is not what I came for, I was sent to slay a beast."

"Is a sickness that turns little children into the undead not monstrous enough for you?"

"I've never taken an innocent life."

He stepped forwards and gazed into my eyes. "I can see it," he said.

"See what?"

"The darkness inside you. You've got more than enough to do what I ask."

I shook my head. "I'm sorry." I began to walk away. I'd report my findings to Hellwyn, see what she wanted to do about it.

And then I felt his hand on the back of my raincoat. His eyes were dark now. Like flint. "You'll slay this monster. It's what you were sent to do. Do it now, before I have to force your hand."

"Force my hand?" What was he going to do, pull a pen from his pocket and stab me with it?

"I've studied the arcane arts. I can transform, if only for a short while. I can become something else...."

I shrugged his hand off and strode toward the door but the air began to shift around me. The temperature plummeted. I turned back as he began to shout.

"You came to slay a beast? Then a beast I will be." A dense cloud of magic swirled around him and the dark eddies mimicked the worms that wriggled across his forehead.

The spell he was conjuring was one of transformation, but it was like nothing I'd ever seen. The billowing magic that surrounded him swirled faster and faster, and formed menacing shapes.

Wolves.

He spoke in strange tongues and began to grunt like a savage. Fur erupted from his face, throat and hand. Thick, wild lustrous brown and grey fur.

His eyes narrowed and shifted as his face elongated into a snout and his glasses clattered to the ground. He threw his head back to reveal long, curved, wicked, ivory fangs. A dry tearing sound came from his suit as his body became wracked with spasms. Fur jutted from the holes in his clothes and his eyes glowed yellow around his black sliver-like pupils. "A pity you pushed me to this." His voice was low and hoarse. Primal. Long black claws sprouted from his fingers.

He grabbed a flaming torch from the wall and threw it onto the bench beside his children, splattering them with hot pitch. Within moments the flames danced and spread across their clothes.

I couldn't watch, and as I turned away, I found him stalking towards me, the man gone and in his place, a beast.

- THIRTY ONE -

I unsheathed my sword as the monster raked its paw through the air, faster than I could move. Firelight glinted on each of the curled black claws that descended towards me.

I stumbled back as its claws raked at my chest. The raincoat shimmered and the beast roared, snatching its paw away as pain and bewilderment twisted its monstrous face.

I held the sword like a silver barrier between us.

Kill.

The hilt trembled in my hand as I focused my intention but images of the man he'd been and the children he'd lost flashed through my mind. I shut them away, took a step back, and steadied my grip on the sword as the monster leapt at me. The blade glinted as I swung it toward the creature's thick, furry throat.

The wolf smacked the blade with a great paw and howled as it sunk into its flesh. Hot red blood spattered my face as it wrenched its hand away. Its growl was low and feral as it stalked in a slow deliberate arc, its eyes gleamed and its teeth gnashed in fury.

I prepared myself for the onslaught, but the creature cradled its paw beneath its armpit and bounded away, shouldering the remains of the door off its hinges and vanishing into the shadows.

Heat blazed at my back. The conflagration roared and spat across the chamber, engulfing the benches and turning the three tiny lifeless figures into bright red orange dolls of fire.

I fled from the burning room as a mournful howl echoed through the tunnels above. The stairs were splattered with drops of steaming blood. I ran up, taking them two at a time as snakes of black smoke swirled behind me.

Where was he? I scoured the gloom for a sign of the beast, but he was gone.

Paw prints were scattered through the dirt and dust. I ran, following them until a stitch pricked my side, forcing me to stop.

I leaned over to catch my breath and strained to hear the beast's movement. The place was silent but for the occasional drip of water from the caverns above.

Once again I found myself reaching for my bag. "No crystals, no gun." I needed magic, and fast. I closed my eyes and reached out, hoping to tap into any mystical pockets of energy that might dwell in this dark, forsaken place.

The place sizzled with magic, it thrummed through the cold stone walls. I reached out to the ancient rock tunnel and shivered as the power buzzed through my hand.

It washed through every part of my being, quenching a long aching thirst. I trembled like a lost man in the desert who's finally found an oasis. The sheer abundance of power was almost overwhelming.

But it was a dark magic.

It twisted through me and reached into the core of my being, searching for something I'd long suppressed. The darkness within.

I stood tall, my muscles rippling, my senses more alive than they'd ever been. I felt invincible. And starved for destruction. My very being screamed to burn up the power coursing through me. I ran, my footsteps hard and fast as I thundered through the tunnel. I had quarry to pursue. My mind delighted at the prospect of facing the beast and basking in my own darkness, as I rose to the challenge of slaying it.

Show me.

Rings of light glowed on the ground, highlighting a trail of large scarlet footprints amongst the scurry of boot marks.

I tracked them to a side tunnel where a cold shrieking wind cut through the air. It brought a riot of scents; grassy and floral. A vision of towering trees and the wide open skies that lay beyond this lost city filled my mind. The Hinterlands proper. It promised adventure but I had no desire to pursue it. My only objective was to smash my foe to the ground.

He was still among the ruins, hiding in the shadows, his instinct for survival overriding the plea to end his tragic, pitiful life.

I ran, slowing as I followed the beast's footprints as they descended down a flight of stairs.

A low growl rumbled ahead.

A warning.

A challenge.

Light. The magic pulsed through me and I conjured a fireball in the palm of my hand, just bright enough to light my way. It crackled and spat as I tossed it ahead. The flames glowed and pulsed through the air, illuminating the dark tunnel and exposing my quarry.

He was stooped over a pile of chalk white bones, the remains of some creature far viler than him. A feral growl echoed along the tunnel as the ball of fire struck the wall behind him. The flames spread across the stone and his eyes glowed almost as bright as he threw back his head and howled.

Then he charged.

The ground rumbled and his claws scraped the stony ground. He ran on all fours, limping where my sword had slashed his palm. Dust rained from above and each step rattled the floor like an earthquake.

He was a man once. A lost soul. Just like me. I shook my head to quash the thought. It was weak. Unnecessary. I raised the blade, my mind perfectly focused upon one intent.

Kill.

My heart beat like a drum as he thundered towards me, his face wracked with hatred and fury. He bounded and leaped, claws outstretched.

I threw myself back to the ground. The air rushed and whistled as he flew over me and smashed into the stone wall. I leaped to my feet and brought my sword up as he bounded again.

Claws and steel clashed, and sparks flew as he raked the coat's enchanted armor. I shifted my grip on the hilt as he raised a giant paw to strike, then I lunged forward, driving the blade deep into his chest.

His paw struck my face with a limp, winded, dying force but it was still powerful enough to knock me to the ground. Scorching hot agony seared the side of my face.

The beast groaned, the sound disconcertingly human as his transformation began to fall away. Half wolf, half man. His eyes were human now and filled with agony and terror. "End it." he said, his voice hoarse and pleading. He coughed, sending a stream of blood down his lightly furred chin. "End me."

His humanity quelled the darkness inside me and it began to ebb away as I staggered towards him. I tried not to meet his eyes but a terrible gurgle escaped his lips as I wrenched the sword free.

"Please..." He growled. "Just-"

The sword swept in an arc of steel, severing his head just as it had his wife's. It sailed through the air, struck the tunnel wall and thumped to the ground as a geyser of blood erupted from his throat.

I sheathed the sword and stumbled away. My mind and system were numb with horror and pain, as well as an unexpected yearning for the powerful darkness that had consumed me.

- THIRTY TWO -

The tunnels were quiet as I walked back. I felt low and empty but that void soon filled with dark melancholy. The opposite of how I'd expected to feel after having bested Hellwyn's beast.

I glanced over the footprints in the dust, mine were easy enough to spot among the other strange markings, especially with the heavy tread on the soles of my boots. I followed my tracks and kept an eye on Hellwyn's necklace. Soon it brightened and I began to recognize some of the turns I'd taken, as well as some of the oddly shaped formations of fungus pulsing on the walls. Then I found the headless zombie. I retched as I looked away from the undeniable waypoint.

Fighting zombies should have been all in a night's work for me, but I'd known this one. Or at least I was aware of her tragic past. And her children's. They were probably little more than charred bone by now and I struggled to shake that image out of my head as I staggered on.

I was on full alert as I slowly climbed the stairs that led up out of the deeps and emerged in the corridor where Hellwyn's refuge was hidden. The necklace blazed with light and I found the chalk-like runes that marked the entrance. I stood before the wall, took a deep breath and stepped through, into the light and safety of the room beyond.

"So the deed is done?" Hellwyn sat upon her pirate chest sharpening a knife with a whetstone. "You've slain the beast?"

I slumped down on the edge of the bed and stared at the ground for a moment, before telling her what had happened.

"It's a sad story," Hellwyn said. "But you'd hear countless more if you spent any significant time in the Hinterlands. Are you sure the sickness he spoke of is contained?" She asked the question casually but I heard the undercurrent of concern.

"Yes. They're all dead."

"You're wounded. Were you bitten?"

I shook my head.

"Good." Hellwyn continued to stare at me. "You seem different, changed. Did you run across anything else in the tunnels?"

"No." But my thoughts had jumped straight to that overwhelming cloud of dark magic that had reached into my core and found its match inside me.

"Right." Hellwyn stood, slipped the knife into a hidden sheath inside her shirt and dropped the whetstone into the chest. "So, you survived all on your own, without your bag of tricks and magic crystals?"

"Not exactly. I found magic down there. And I used it."

She smiled. "Hmm. It seems strange that someone as unskilled... as non magical as you claim to be, could have gotten command over it. And yet you've used it and it barely seems to have left a mark upon you. Has it ever occurred to you that whoever convinced you that you couldn't use magic properly was lying?"

"No, I-"

"How were you recruited into the Organization?"

"Underwood. My boss, he found me. Kind of." I rubbed my

hands over my knees. "I left home when I was eighteen and lived on the streets until I met this guy Darrow. He helped me, gave me a place to crash, actually bothered to listen to me and teach me stuff I needed to know. Up until that point I didn't have much of a clue about magic."

"Really?" Hellwyn sounded doubtful.

"No. I mean I kind of knew I was different."

"How so?"

"Sometimes I'd get pissed off, especially at school and things would happen. Weird things. Stupid things. Once, I remember wishing the teacher would just vanish and she did. It was only for a few seconds but it caused total havoc. My foster dad went berserk and grounded me for months. It wasn't my fault, I wasn't in control but after that I just tried like hell to be as normal as possible. At least until I left."

"Why did you leave?"

"My foster father had a girlfriend. A total bitch. She got weird with me one night, tried it on. I told her to go fuck herself. She didn't like the rejection so she set me up, made out that I'd stolen her engagement ring."

"And did you?"

"No. Like I said, she set me up. My dad went crazy and kicked me out, so I ended up in the city. That's when I met Darrow. He was kind of shifty. Actually..." I laughed and couldn't help but smile, thinking about the crazy shit we'd gotten up to over that seemingly endless summer of mayhem. "he was an out and out criminal, but that's another story. Darrow. Darrow showed me the city's magical quarters, and taught me some pretty underhanded tricks. Once I realized magic was real and that most people knew nothing about it, I felt like I was shooting fish in a barrel. We ran wild across the city and set up all kinds of scams."

"Until you were caught."

"Yeah. We got busted by the Organization. That's when I met Underwood. He gave me a choice, take his job offer or go to Stardim. He'd even offered a wage, of sorts...it seemed great, like a real no brainer but that's just how it goes, when you're eighteen and clueless."

"And the Organization trained you?" Hellwyn watched me intently now.

"Yeah. They taught me how to fight, mixed arts, mainly defensive. Then they assigned a mage. That's when I found out how little I knew about magic, it was a frustrating experience, painful really. For both of us. Eventually he changed tack, showed me how to be covert and how to get by with their various amulets and gadgets." I ran a hand over my shoulder bag, glad to have it back. I stopped as Hellwyn smiled. "They taught me what I needed to know, enough to round up criminals and scumbags. Enough to be their *odd job man*. Which was fine by me, I needed something to do and the work was interesting. To say the least."

"And so you became the Organization's pawn."

"What have you got against them?"

"They're dishonest," Hellwyn said.

"And mercenaries are honorable?"

"It's not about honor, it's about truth. I don't pretend to answer a higher calling. Not anymore. Like I said, the Organization's the hand of the Council, and the Council's intentions are as murky as shit."

"I wouldn't know."

"You seem to enjoy being kept in the dark."

I said nothing. She wasn't entirely wrong. Ignorance felt...easier, or at least it had, up until this point.

"You can only bury your head in the sand for so long. I was the same," Hellwyn said. "I did my work, took the money, didn't ask questions. But then the killings started and the city changed..."

"Everything's been so extreme lately."

She nodded. "Things are coming to a head."

"Maybe you should put some faith in the Organization. They're trying to stop the murders."

"Are they?" Hellwyn's eyes were as hard as stone now.

So I've been told. I thought back to the bounty hunters waiting in the office on the morning Tom had been killed. The truth was, I had no idea what was going on. Up until then, it had suited me to live day to day, my only concern hunting down Elsbeth Wyght and putting a bullet in her skull. Now it seemed like all these unspoken truths were coming out and my world was turning upside down, whether I wanted it to or not. "The man...the one I killed in the tunnels said he smelled many worlds on me. Do you know what he meant?"

"Do you know where you were born?" Hellwyn asked.

I shrugged. "Anything prior to the age of ten is a black hole."

"You said Tom was around for you as long as you can remember."

"He was." *And maybe even before that.* I thought of the dream I'd had, of the otherworld, of the cave, and of Tom. I held my tongue.

"Curious..." She looked like she was about to say more when a tiny frown creased her brow.

"What?"

Hellwyn shook her head and fastened the belt by her side. "We can talk later. Right now, we need to take action. You've proven yourself to be of use, so let's put you to it."

"I'm flattered."

"Just do as I say and maybe we'll both survive. Then, once we've stopped the assassin, we can look deeper into the mystery of Morgan Rook. Right?"

"Sure." I pulled my gun and holster from my bag and strapped it over my shoulder. "So where are we going?"

"Back to your world."

"And then?"

"We need to have a talk with some people who are about as keen to be out in the open as I am. But the more of us the better."

"Who are they?"

"They're all that's left of the Order."

"What's the Order?"

"We were a circle of fighters. Knights. That's about all you need to know."

"Listen," I tried to keep my irritation from my voice, "If we're going to work together..."

Hellwyn sighed. "There were nine of us, we worked as a unit. This was a long time ago, longer than I care to remember. We were an Order, a secret society if you will. Our purpose was simple; to protect our king, queen and country. We rid the capital of crime and disorder, not unlike how the Organization purports to work."

"Where was this?"

"A city far from here. But that doesn't matter, you asked about the Order and I'm trying to tell you what you want to know." She let out an ambivalent sigh. "We were united, indomitable until everything changed. It happened when the king and queen lost their firstborn. They'd have done anything to get their princess back, and they summoned a death cult to the palace. Its leader was successful, he brought their daughter back from the dead." Hellwyn's smile turned to a grimace. "We knew it was wrong, and time proved us right. First servants began to disappear, then children. We searched high and low for them, and one day we found them in the cellars, their bodies rotting, mauled, chunks of flesh missing." She shook her head.

"What happened?"

"The king's daughter. I followed her. She was wily, fast. She slayed a serving boy and dragged him down into her lair to feed. I found what was left of his remains and told the queen. At first it seemed she'd refused to accept it, but later I realized she'd believed my every word. Soon after, her daughter vanished, and then the king summoned the Order. He commanded us to round up the cult and make them answer for what they'd done, but they'd fled in the night. It took us three long years to track them down, and when we did...we slaughtered them. Every single last one of them..." her voice faltered. "We struck like assassins in the night and killed them where they slept."

I thought back to the assassin, how it had slain Tom and the voice that had whispered in its mind. *Sleep, old man. Sleep like those you slaughtered.* "Was that the end of it?"

"No, if only. Once we'd eliminated the cult, the queen decided our heads must roll, lest any of us tell the tale of her undead daughter. Of course we would have kept our word, but the queen was utterly unbalanced by that time. So we disbanded and scattered to the wind. Tom fled to your world and eventually we joined him and reunited." Hellwyn's smile was bittersweet. "Things were okay at first, but after awhile we all began to drift apart. I kept in contact with Tom but eventually he discovered booze and took to it with aplomb, mostly I'm sure to silence the guilt."

"Guilt for what?"

"Didn't you hear what I said? We murdered people, killed them in their sleep. Loathsome people, but people none the less." Tears pricked her eyes. She wiped them away and her cheeks blazed with anger. "We had to do it. There was no other choice. The cult was playing with things that should have been left well alone, summoning all sorts of dark forces. I tried to tell Tom this over and over but he couldn't accept it."

"I saw it. What happened to him." I said. "He barely fought back. It was almost as if he'd given in to the assassin."

"He thought he deserved to die. Maybe he did. Maybe we all do."

"Could anyone from the cult have survived?"

"No. They were eliminated, all of them. I'm certain of it."

"Someone wants revenge, and the way this assassin leaves the bodies...like they're-"

"Sleeping." Hellwyn's voice was low. "I know, but it doesn't make sense. No one could have followed us to your world. No one knew where we went. It can't be related."

"What about someone from the Order? Would any of them have mentioned where you'd gone?"

"No one would have said a..." She gave me a hard look and folded her arms.

It seemed she wasn't going to add anything further so I decided to try another tack. "Right. Well, let's find the remaining members and see what they know."

"One of them has been trying to contact me. Prentice. Up to now I've ignored his calls. I had no wish to see him, but I'll contact him now."

"I'm assuming it won't be through anything as simple as a telephone?"

Hellwyn smiled. "You're getting the gist of this, aren't you?" She held up her hand and pointed to a ring with a large oval of quartz set in the center. "If anyone lights the candle in the graveyard, the flame's reflected here, inside the stone. Green for the Order, amber for strangers. If we light our own candle, the others will receive our signal. I'll go and see if I can summon Prentice. Providing he's still alive."

Hellwyn blew out the oil lamps and lantern, plunging the room into darkness. And then she grabbed my wrist. "Come. Let's find the survivors of my poor dying Order, while there's still time."

- THIRTY THREE -

We stepped through the wall and emerged in the tunnel.

This time it wasn't empty.

Two figures strode towards us. The first raised a hand, palm out. Hellwyn did the same. It was hard to see much below the figure's hood, but I could just about make out a young man with tired eyes and a wolfish grin. Behind him, a woman with a pale face and deep black eyes. My heart beat hard as she smiled, and whispered, "Be safe." Her words were warm but there was an underlying hint of something below them. A faint perfume surrounded her, making me think of cherries and wintry mornings. Then she and her companion passed us by and vanished into the gloom.

"Who were they?" I asked.

"Fellow travelers."

"Do you know them?" I still felt intoxicated by the woman's perfume and the memory of her smile.

"I've seen them around. Best not to pay too much attention to those you meet in the Hinterlands. Everyone has their purpose for being here, some benign, some not. Come on."

We continued along the tunnel and Hellwyn checked her compass. She marched on a little further, stopped, and shone her light upon a long narrow band of glass set into the black rock wall. Hellwyn rapped her fingers upon it.

I glanced through the strange window, to see what lay between this eerie half world and the ones beyond it. It looked like a soup of stars and distant comets. Then a face reared into view.

A Gloaming Ghast. His dark, empty eyes found mine and he thumped a finger upon the glass, producing the sound of depth charges.

I backed off and looked away, anywhere to escape its eyes.

"This way." Hellwyn strode on. She checked her compass again and finally stopped. Her light shone upon the wall, revealing a large, oval glass that twinkled within the stone. She rapped upon it and listened.

Silence.

"It's free of Gloaming Ghasts. You go first. Be quick."

"What do I do?"

"Walk into the glass and think of home."

"That's it? Should I click my shoes as well?"

"Just do as I said. Quickly!" Hellwyn shoved me in the back and I fell forward.

The glass enveloped me and I began to fall, white stars and comets bursting around me. I did my best to ignore my rising panic, concentrating on an image of my apartment and the army of hungry cats waiting to be fed. Sound roared in my ears and the whole world seemed to turn on its head as I tumbled through the juddering space around me.

The temperature rose from icy cold to warm and I found myself falling out of the liquid-like glass and into a room.

I froze.

Seven figures stood before me. They stared, stunned. Most were naked, their tan bodies bent into bizarre, unnatural configurations. The others wore a hodgepodge of strange, unmatched clothes.

Mannequins.

I looked around to find myself in a thrift store, a tall dusty mirror behind me.

The glass rippled like water and a loud crackle followed as Hellwyn stepped through the mirror. She glanced around and smiled "We're not too far from my house." She led me through the shadowy store. The shelves teemed with people's unwanted junk, steeped in dust and memories from a jumbled grab-bag of different eras. My phone rumbled in my pocket. The screen was blinding in the depths of the dark store. The message must have been sent while I was roaming through the Hinterlands.

- DH- THERE'S BEEN ANOTHER MURDER.

- THIRTY FOUR -

I deleted Haskins' message as Hellwyn drew alongside me. "What is it?" she asked.

"There's been another murder. I'm sorry."

"And then there were two..." Hellwyn sighed. "Me, and...whoever else is left. I feel like I'm living on borrowed time. Do you know who it was?"

"Give me a minute, I'll call my contact." The shop door was bolted but Hellwyn unlocked it with a wave of her hand and I slipped out onto the street.

Dawn crept over the city and a cool chill laced the air. Haskins picked up on the third ring. "I take it you want details."

I tried to ignore the oily greed in his voice. "I need everything you've got on the victim, including location."

"Early sixties. Her body was found in a house on the north side of town. I'll send you the address from my burner. As far as suspects are concerned, we've got sweet FA, asides from-"

"Okay, anything else on the victim." I looked up and down the empty street.

"Cracked the case have you?" Haskins' voice was thick with mockery, but also curiosity. "What have you got?"

"Nothing that'll help your investigation...this isn't something the department is going to be able to...deal with."

"Just tell me-"

"If you want the kickback, I need the address. Pronto."

Hellwyn emerged as I hung up. She quietly closed the shop door and ran a hand over the lock until it clicked. She looked cowed and sad, but as she turned to face me she straightened up and her face resumed its usual stony composure.

I told her what I knew.

"Clara." She shook her head. "I never dreamed I'd outlive her." She stared into the gutter, her finger playing over the pommel of her sword. "That leaves Prentice."

"Prentice?"

"He was the last to join the Order and the first to leave it."

"Where is he?"

Hellwyn shrugged. "Who knows? He left us almost as soon as we arrived in this world. Clearly he saw the potential for wealth here. Gold's always been a color to catch his eye." Hellwyn glanced at the sky, her face unreadable. "I'll summon him. Come on."

The city was quiet and still as we walked through the streets, as if we were the last living souls in this world. Then a cab came into view and Hellwyn hailed it down.

If the driver noticed our strange clothes or the swords under our coats, he showed no sign. We rode in silence, staring pensively through the windows until we arrived at the square.

By day the graveyard seemed larger, like a great desolate jungle of brambles and grass. Hellwyn paid the cab driver. He gazed from her to me, then the graveyard. He touched a golden crucifix hanging from his mirror, made the sign of the cross and then sped away.

"Come on." Hellwyn opened the gate and led me down a path through the tall weeds that had sprung up among the chipped and broken gravestones. The place was eerily silent, especially for a place in the city: no birds in the trees, no scurrying rats and mice.

Hellwyn stopped before the angel, placed her hand gently on its stone arm and lit the candle. The flame danced and burned in a bright shade of red that threw an unearthly light over the angel's cupped hands.

"What now?" I asked.

Hellwyn sat on a weather-beaten bench and nodded for me to join her. "Now we wait."

. . .

We sat and spoke for what seemed like hours until I heard footsteps crunching on gravel. A crow cawed, as if heralding the new arrival, a man with slicked back hair and a smart black suit. He walked towards us slowly, cautiously, his dark eyes narrowing as they roved over Hellwyn and growing distinctly colder as they found me.

I hated him at first sight.

"And you are?" Hellwyn asked, her voice friendly even as her hand slipped casually beneath her coat, no doubt clutching her sword.

I scoured the brush to see if there were others, but he appeared to be alone.

"My name is Ashcombe, I work for Prentice Sykes." His voice held a trace of an accent, but from where I had no idea. He smiled disarmingly at Hellwyn, before gesturing to me. "And your friend?"

"Irrelevant," Hellwyn said.

"Very well." The sunlight caught his silver monogrammed cufflinks as he extended his hand to Hellwyn. They spelled out 'Shhh'.

Hellwyn remained stock still, ignoring his gesture.

"Well, pleased to finally meet you Hellwyn. Mr. Sykes has been attempting to contact you for some time now. He wishes to speak with you regarding a most urgent matter and," his eyes strayed to me, "a most private one. Now, if you'll come with me." He gestured to the path he'd appeared from.

I didn't like this at all, but Hellwyn seemed unfazed. She turned to me. "Go to my house, wait for me. There's a spare key on the lintel over the door. Not that you'll need it. I shouldn't be long."

"I don't trust him." I didn't even bother to lower my voice. Ashcombe could go to hell for all I cared. Puffed up little prick.

He glared at me, then turned back to Hellwyn. "My employer will only see you if you come on your own. Is that a problem? Because if you feel you need a bodyguard to accompany you, I'll have to contact Mr. Sykes before we can proceed."

"I don't need a bodyguard," Hellwyn said, her voice laced with anger. Her eyes softened as she glanced back at me. "I have to see Prentice; if these are his terms then so be it."

"Follow me." Ashcombe slipped on a pair of expensive-looking sunglasses and strode away.

"See you soon." Hellwyn gave me a brief, tight smile before turning to follow Ashcombe through the graveyard.

I stood and watched them vanish amid the foliage, my instincts screaming at me to follow.

"Screw it," I mumbled, and took off after them.

- THIRTY FIVE -

I followed from a distance and watched from the graveyard as they opened the gate and stood beside a silver Jaguar E-type convertible. The sight of the car jarred me, and it was only once Hellwyn had climbed inside, that I realized why.

I'd seen it before, parked in that shadowy alley on the night that Tom had been attacked by those thugs.

As I ran towards the gate, Ashcombe started the engine and the car purred to life. Then his sunglasses flashed as he glanced in the mirror and drove away.

"Shit."

By the time I got to the street they were long gone.

As I leaned over to catch my breath, I caught the flash of Hellwyn's pendant glowing beneath my shirt. I pulled it out and scoured the square, desperate for a means to follow them.

A man stood outside his house. A kid waved to him from the upstairs window but he paid no attention while he fished through his pockets with one hand and balanced a motorbike helmet on the handlebars with his other.

Perfect.

"Morning," I said, giving the man a wide, disarming smile.

He looked me up and down with dull suspicious eyes as he finally found his keys. "What do you want?"

"I'd like to borrow your bike."

"Go fuc-"

"Listen." I placed a hand on his shoulder and gazed into his piggy eyes. "I really want to borrow your bike, and you *really* want to lend me it."

"I...I'm not sure." He looked doubtful. It was enough.

"Don't worry." I reached into my bag, pulled out a pouch and dropped it into his hand. "I understand. Trust's a two-way street. Here's a bag of gold. Enough to buy you a whole garage full of expensive toys. You look after it while I'm gone and if I don't come back, you get to keep it. Right?"

His face lit up as he opened the pouch and a golden light spilled out. "Wow!"

Wow indeed. For now at least. Less so later.

The man continued to gaze into the pouch as I took the keys and slipped the helmet over my head. It was a perfect fit.

I straddled the bike, put it in neutral, squeezed the clutch and started it up. The engine roared into life, thrumming below me as a blue cloud of exhaust billowed up.

The bike was fast. It jolted around the square and out into the street beyond. But there was no sign of Hellwyn or Ashcombe.

I pulled over, grabbed a crystal and closed my eyes. "Show me the car". I conjured the image of the silver Jaguar into my mind, before opening my eyes.

A trace of the car hung in the air, a faint blurred silver line like a time-lapse image, and it pointed me in the direction they'd gone. I opened up the throttle, swept out into the road, and sped towards the distant intersection, the bike roaring like a metallic beast.

Despite the early hour, traffic was already getting bad. I wove in and out of the lanes trying to get around the slower cars and trucks. The bike was sleek but heavier than I expected, but soon riding it became second nature. I gunned it and searched for lingering traces of the silver Jag, and for a moment I got lost in the pursuit.

The horn of a semi-truck blared. I looked up to see its grille thundering towards me. I swerved round it, narrowly avoiding a school bus.

"Moron!" someone shouted.

I couldn't argue with that. And then I spotted the Jag up ahead. I slowed, pulled in behind an SUV and left a few cars in between me and my quarry.

The traffic crawled, but eventually it began to thin as we neared the outskirts of the city and drove along the coast. I held back as the Jaguar sped down the highway. It seemed to be heading back inland towards the rolling, forested hills in the distance.

I hadn't been out this way in a long time and as I looked at the trees, a low, cold feeling passed through me.

It was a bad omen.

- THIRTY SIX -

Somewhere, on the summit of one of those hills, was a dark rambling place. The place I'd been born, aged ten.

I felt sick.

The Jaguar sped through the early autumn leaves and they curled up and flew around its sleek silver body. I slowed, let a few cars pass and hoped to the Gods that Ashcombe hadn't noticed me. He turned at a crossroads, taking a heavily forested road. I fell back and followed slowly.

When I reached the turn, the road stretching before me was empty. I sped up, taking the tight bends with caution, expecting to see his car. But I didn't.

I gunned the engine and swept up the hill but it soon became clear that I'd lost them.

"Shit," my voice echoed inside the helmet. I pulled over. "Shit, shit shit."

I scanned the road for a sign of Ashcombe's car, but there was nothing. I rubbed the back of my aching neck and my finger connected with a chain. Hellwyn's pendant. I pulled it out from my shirt. It was dim but at least there was something.

It was a familiar. Ashcombe's familiar. Or had been. He'd cut it loose for some reason, rejected it. And now it was insane with anger and fear. I recalled the silver cufflinks gleaming on his shirt sleeve. *Shhh.*

I held my sword between us as it shambled closer, its huge eyes blinking rapidly. An insect crawled from its lips, some tiny black many-legged creature.

It was almost upon me. I swung the sword, my intent set on cleaving the misshapen head from that cursed body. It jumped back with surprising speed and my sword bit into a tree.

I fought to pull the blade free as the monster lurched at me, I let go of the hilt and fell back to avoid the swipe of its talons.

I struggled to free my gun, which was caught in its holster. I fired two quick rounds. The grip juddered in my slick gritty palm. I didn't hear the shots. Nor their impact. Or the screams escaping its lips as it clapped its hands over its ears. But both shots found their mark. One in its chest, one in its shoulder. They oozed and leaked piss-colored blood.

My feet skidded across the leaves as I scrambled to my feet and backed away, bringing the gun up as it threw back its head and spat. I closed my eyes, my howl of agony silent. Venom seared my eyelids.

It stank of bile and decay, its viscous glue-like film, leaving me both blind and deaf.

- THIRTY SEVEN -

I crawled away and rubbed my eyes, my fingers burning from the phlegm. I dug in my bag for a vial of blessed water and rinsed and rubbed my eyes with it until I could open them enough to see the familiar lumbering towards me. A single, pointed yellowed tooth gleamed in its mouth.

It took another swipe, the tip of a claw found my temple and sliced it open. I leaped up as it drew back its hand for another strike and kneed it in the stomach.

Its grey leathery flesh was horribly unyielding and the creature inside its belly kicked back as the monster leaned over, its mouth wide with yellow liquid dripping from its lips.

I ran to the tree where my sword hung and grabbed the hilt. It was slick with sweat but I clenched it with both hands and pulled with all my might.

The blade jerked free. I spun round, dancing aside as the monster lunged towards me, and stumbled into the tree. A heavy branch cracked beneath my boot as I stepped back. The creature grimaced.

The sound.

It didn't like the sound. It pained it, riled it.

I waited for it to lunge again and smacked the flat of the blade against a tree trunk. The beast faltered and brought its long hands up over its ears.

I struck the tree again and it clenched its hands harder to its head. Then I swung the blade and opened its throat. It clamped both hands to the wound, its huge eyes staring with unfettered hatred. I slammed the sword against the tree again and the vile creature threw its hands back to its ears.

I swung the sword with one intent.

It slipped through the wound in its throat, plunging deeper, biting through sinew and bone. My sense of hearing was restored as its head struck the ground with a wet, solid thud.

I wanted to leave the thing where it lay but my training nagged me to cover it up. I scanned the forest for its lair. There was a cave nearby, the creature's treasure trove. Deep inside was a small mountain of bleached bones, the remains of past victims. People who had made the mistake of trespassing on this land. Adults. Kids. All dead and gone, their bones keepsakes for this hideous creature.

I dragged the headless body through the leaves, down into the darkness of its earthy den and returned for the head. It made a satisfying thump as I kicked it through the air and watched it bounce and tumble down into the mouth of the cave.

If I made it out of here, I'd have to let Dauple know where it was. Finding it would totally make his day.

I climbed the hill with one hand on my sword.

The trees seemed to loom over me as I neared the house and the atmosphere reeked of malevolence and dark energy. I paused to scan the perimeter with my telescope.

All the blinds were drawn with the exception of a large picture window that dominated most of the building's upper floor. I could see Hellwyn inside, facing a small, bearded man who must have been in his early sixties. Prentice Sykes, I assumed.

Their conversation appeared to be cordial enough and it seemed she wasn't under any immediate threat, despite the malignancy that surrounded the place.

I crept through the trees, keeping low to avoid the attention of any watchful eyes as I made my way toward the back of the house.

A short stony walkway led to a stout wooden door. The air prickled with magic. Deep, dark, evil magic. Its intensity was almost hypnotic. Bad stuff had happened here, very bad stuff. Dangerous things summoned, things best left alone.

I thought of calling Underwood, but the signal was bad, too much interference. It was hardly surprising given the black magic that teemed in the air. I was tempted to tap into that energy, to let it power me up but my gut instinct told me I wanted no part of it.

I tried the door. It was locked. I reached into my bag and pulled out a charged crystal. The energy inside was so docile compared to the magic swelling from the house, but it was clean and light. And it would do. I squeezed it and took in every last drop before reaching for the lock.

Blazing heat shot through my hand. I winced and pulled away.

Cursed. Another attempt to unlock it with magic could be fatal.

At least I had my petty crime skills to fall back on. I rummaged through my lock picks and made a careful selection. Within moments the lock clicked and I pulled on my iron-laced gloves to shield myself from the worst of the hex and prevent it from affecting me.

I took a deep breath and opened the door onto a hallway lined with shadows. I could see a faint gleam of light illuminating a distant flight of stairs. I closed the door behind me and crept down the hall.

Artful black and white photographs hung on the walls; mountains, forests, beaches. All elegantly framed and signed in the corner. The owner of this house had taste as well as money.

Black spots swarmed before my eyes as I passed a closed room. Something heavy lurked behind the door. Something that made the familiar who had stalked the forest outside look like the tooth fairy.

Voices and laughter rang down from upstairs, Hellwyn's deep tone muffled through the ceiling. The pace of her words sounded calm, but as I reached the foot of the stairs the conversation ended, along with all the sound in the world.

As if someone had hit the mute button once more.

My skin crawled. The spell of silence hadn't belonged solely to the familiar, it was the hallmark of its master.

I spun round as a cosh descended towards me. Darkness exploded before my eyes and I fell through the floor, down down into endless night.

- THIRTY EIGHT -

The darkness was restless. It crept and crawled like shiny black beetles as cold air swept over me, bringing scents I'd never smelled and flavors I'd never tasted before.

A wind from another world.

I caught dark scents, fire, death, suffering. This world was not a place I wanted to know. An emptiness loomed behind me. A giant canvas of black paint that shifted. I'd seen this before.

I'd been...inside it. No. *Through* it. Light flickered around the periphery of my vision and as I blinked, it grew as bright as daylight.

I opened my eyes again.

"My apologies," a man said.

I found myself lying on a sofa in the room where I'd seen Hellwyn. Behind me loomed the huge window I'd spotted from the forest. The man, who I took to be Prentice Sykes, stood over me holding a glass of water in one hand and a glass of wine in the other. Despite his diminutive stature, he was strong, powerful, not someone to trifle with. His grey tailored suit probably cost more than I'd made that year.

I took the glass of water and sipped it before setting it onto the coffee table. The back of my head thrummed with pain. I rubbed it as I slowly looked around the room. Hellwyn stood before a tall shelf filled with oversized art books. She looked angry and...worried?

"What happened?" I asked. I leaned forward slowly and took another sip of water.

The bearded man smiled. "Ashcombe happened."

As if on cue, the weaselly little prick entered the room and gave me a long look of loathing. "We don't take well to trespassers."

"Yeah," I agreed. "I got that impression after your familiar tried to add me to its collection of bones."

"Familiar?" Hellwyn's voice was calm but her eyes grew wide and she looked at me, as if she was trying to tell me something. We're in danger? Yeah, that much was already crystal clear.

"Yes, his familiar," I said. "A goat-faced creature with a writhing belly full of who knows what. It was powerful as familiars go." I glanced at the bearded man. "Was it his, or yours?"

He shook his head and took a sip of wine. "Not mine, no. I'm Prentice by the way." He held out a well-manicured hand and shook mine. Apparently the discussion of demonic familiars had concluded.

I tried to read him as best I could as we shook hands, but there was nothing there. I'd been stonewalled. A fat band of gold encircled his forefinger, perhaps something inside it was blocking my attempts to assess him.

"I understand you're helping Hellwyn with our...mutual friend," Prentice said.

I nodded, but kept my eye on Ashcombe until he'd left the room. "It seems odd to call an assassin that's slaughtered your partners...a friend." My arm lurched as my thoughts jumped to my weapons, my bag. They were gone. I glanced at Hellwyn, she still had her sword.

"It's just a turn of phrase, Mr. Rook." Prentice drained his wine and picked out a bottle of something dark and expensive looking from the liquor cabinet behind him. "A top up?"

I shook my head and winced as another wave of pain washed over me. "I'm alright with water, thanks."

Prentice refilled Hellwyn's glass and then his own, before lifting it to toast her. "To old friends, those who have passed and those who remain."

Hellwyn's smile was forced as she took a sip.

This was all wrong. The contrived bonhomie, the house. Ashcombe and the wave of evil I'd run into downstairs.

It all felt like....

An endgame.

- THIRTY NINE -

"You mentioned you had an idea of who might be behind the attacks," Hellwyn said to Prentice as she set her wine glass down.

"I have some suspicions." Prentice glanced out the window. "This world's full of threats right now. There's a highly ambitious dark mage gaining traction in the city, perhaps he saw us as adversaries. Then," he paused and smiled at me, "there's that coven. They've been up to all sorts of mayhem, or so I'm told. I expect the Organization's fully aware of the situation. Or maybe they're more of an upper level concern, that our friend here isn't privy too." His voice was slow, languid. As if he were trying to buy time.

For what?

I listened for Ashcombe, but the house was silent.

"A coven, a dark mage," Hellwyn said. There was a low menacing buzz of irritation in her voice. "Really?"

"Why not?" Prentice said. "Either would be more than capable of handling a Hexling."

"And what motive? Why wipe out the Order?" Hellwyn asked. "And how did they find us in the first place?"

"Loose lips sink ships," Prentice said, with another punchably smug grin.

"Loose lips?" Hellwyn's irritation found a harder edge.

Prentice held his glass up. "I enjoy a drink, always have done. As do you. But some of us enjoyed it a bit more than others. Used it to dampen their anguish and guilt. An anguish and guilt which I myself have never felt."

"Get to the point," Hellwyn said. "You're saying Tom got drunk and exposed us?"

"I'm not saying, I'm speculating. Sit, Hellwyn, take the weight off your feet. We need to rest. Recoup our energy before we put serious efforts into finding whoever's behind this"

It was utter bullshit. The man showed no trace of fear or concern. He held all the cards and had time enough to waste. I sat up as something shifted in the air. Prentice glanced my way. Whatever was going to happen seemed to be imminent.

"Where's the bathroom?" I asked, feigning unsteadiness as I climbed to my feet.

"Second door on the right," Prentice said. "Don't be long. We've decisions to make."

I wandered from the room into a short hall with a number of doors and a flight of stairs that led down to the place where Ashcombe had knocked me out. I fumbled loudly with the bathroom door, opened it until it creaked and closed it hard. And then I made my way downstairs as lightly as I could. The air was charged, as if lightning was about to strike. I could feel it all around me.

A ritual was taking place.

Ashcombe.

Shadows seethed across the floor as I crept down the corridor, listening hard. Scratching, tapping and a man's chanting voice slithered from one of the rooms, its cadence twisted and rhythmic. An invocation.

I peered through a crack in the door.

Ashcombe sat cross-legged on the stone floor, encompassed by a chalked circle of glyphs and wards. His eyes were closed, his face intent. He looked so peculiar in his stylish suit, like a businessman conjuring a demon. He wouldn't be the first.

Magic bristled in the air around him. I was tempted to tap in, but it was purely black and evil. A second circle was etched beside him, a dead rabbit lying in the center, its throat leaking viscous blood upon the floor. A sacrifice. An offering.

A savage vibration shook the room. Something was coming.

I ran over and scuffed my foot through the chalk circle, but the symbols remained unmarred. Scalding heat blazed through my shoe and I pulled it back. "Fuck!"

Ashcombe opened his eyes. They were pure ebony, like black holes.

I glanced to the desk behind him. My sword rested below a monitor that ticked with a live feed from the stock market and my bag and coat were draped over an office chair.

Ashcombe grinned as I grabbed them, strapped them on and slipped into my coat. "You have your little bag of borrowed magic, Mr. Rook."

A hiss erupted from the circle and a column of thin grey smoke wafted above the rabbit as it began to twitch and drum its dead paws upon the ground.

A figure appeared in the smoke.

The assassin.

I pulled my gun out and fired at Ashcombe. The bullets struck an unseen force that surrounded him and fell to the floor, flattened and bent.

Ashcombe's malicious grin grew wide as the smoke began to thicken. "This will be interesting." The assassin appeared fully formed. Its dead eyes stared at me from above its mask. Dead, but hideously intent.

I readied my sword. The assassin mirrored me as the smoke around it dissipated.

There was no time to frame my intent. I leapt forward and thrust the sword into the place its heart should be.

The creature parried my blade as if it were nothing more than a twig. My arm jolted with the blow and a crippling ache dogged me as I brought my sword up for another strike.

The assassin beat me to it.

I leaped back, the tip of its blade a hair's breadth from my throat. It followed up with a gloved fist that caught me below the eye. I fell in a crumpled heap and watched helplessly as the creature strode past me and made for the upstairs.

"Hellwyn!" I cried out, but my words were mute as silence fell over the world once more.

I spun round to find Ashcombe still sitting cross legged in his circle, his eyes closed, his face rapt with concentration.

A crossroads, two options. Run up the stairs, or stop Ashcombe before he invoked another ruthless entity. I went for the latter and swung at his head. My sword struck the force field. It rang like a bell.

The din broke his concentration and disrupted his spell.

Ashcombe shot me a look of hatred and resumed the invocation, his lips twitching with a new sense of urgency. I slashed at him again, my sword striking the barrier around him.

Destroy it. I allowed my focus to deepen. An energetic thrum passed from my hand to the grip of my sword. I swung again. This time the blade broke through the barrier and stopped just short of his face.

Ashcombe raised a hand writhing with black flames. They reared up like snakes as he drew back, preparing to throw the malignant curse that swelled from his barbarous core.

He'd have to break his barrier to cast it...

I dropped the sword and delved into my bag, grabbed a crystal and prayed it would have enough power to do what was needed.

Ashcombe's hand swept towards me, the black snake-flames shot out. I reached out and grabbed them, hurling them back before the curse could take hold or the invisible barrier could close.

The crystal in my hand exploded and splinters of quartz cut into my flesh. I dropped the shards as the black curse struck Ashcombe's chest. He grimaced, his manicured hands tearing at his white cotton shirt.

The invisible shield around him flickered away.

I dove for my sword, leaned in and smashed him hard in the face with its pommel.

His breathing grew ragged, his eyes turned from black to white as his head arched back and with one last hideous convulsion he toppled dead to the ground.

Static filled my ears, sounds rushed toward me with a roar and adrenaline shot through my heart as I heard a booming crash upstairs.

- FORTY -

I flew up the stairs, taking them two at a time, my sword gouging plaster from the wall as I ran. Another thundering crash echoed through the room, and I heard Hellwyn's hoarse shout, "You fucking snake!"

The room sizzled with a furious energy as I bolted in.

Hellwyn was poised in the corner, shielded by an overturned bookcase while the assassin stalked towards her.

"Give in. Fighting is futile." Prentice casually swung a sword as he skulked behind the creature's long black cloak.

"I'm going to gut you, you traitorous prick," Hellwyn shouted, then she and Prentice turned toward me.

"That looks like....that's Tom's coat." Prentice brought his blade up. "And why do you have his sword?"

I ignored him and ran at the assassin, my blade high, my intent focused only on separating its head from its neck.

The Hexling barely looked my way as it parried my blow.

I ducked back from the sweep of its sword and lunged again. This time my blade passed through its chest as if it were made of straw.

Foul, noxious vapor streamed into the air as the creature rounded on me and raised its sword for a killing stroke.

I blocked the blow but the force of it sent a shockwave of pain through my wrist and arm.

The assassin's eyes glowed as it pulled its sword away. I stepped in close and stabbed again. The blade plunged through its side, but it did nothing to slow the creature's murderous advance.

Hellwyn came up from behind as it bore down on me, her sword passing in an arc towards the back of its neck. It didn't waver as it threw out its arm to block her assault. Sparks blazed from the armor concealed beneath its simple black cloak.

I lifted my sword to strike but it lunged forward, its fist striking me in the solar plexus and knocking me to the ground.

The assassin spun back to Hellwyn just as she swung again. It parried and tried to follow through with another punch, but she ducked and stabbed up with her blade. It passed through the assassin's arm pit and burst from its shoulder.

Hellwyn let go of the hilt and the assassin fumbled to pull it free as blue-black viscous liquid spilled from the wound.

I scrambled to my feet to assist just as Prentice appeared behind her.

"Hellwyn!" My cry was cut short as her eyes widened and metal glinted through, just under the gentle curve of her chin. Blood sprayed in a fine mist as Prentice pushed his sword deeper still.

Time stopped, and then the world became a blur, a roar. My stomach felt hollow, until it filled with lava and my whole system shook with adrenaline, rage and grief. I stumbled towards Prentice but the assassin blocked my strike, Hellwyn's sword still lodged under its arm. It pulled its fist back and punched me again.

Pain ripped across the side of my face. I went down hard.

Hellwyn still stood. She gave me a calm, resolute look. A trickle of blood ran from her lips, and then she fell. Within moments the trickle became a mournful crimson slick.

I forced myself to my knees and pulled my gun out. I fired at Prentice. My aim was screwed and the bullet clipped his arm. He grimaced and stumbled back, but remained on his feet.

I fired again but the assassin stepped into its path and the round tore through its chest. It stared at me, its eyes dead, its face utterly dispassionate.

"Kill him!" Prentice demanded. But the creature ignored him.

Right. It only had one master. It wasn't Prentice but it was only a matter of time before the command was given, and when it was, I was fucked. Especially in my current state.

I clambered to my feet, grabbed my sword and bolted across the room. There was only one clear way out.

I dove through the window.

Glass exploded and glittered in the air around me as I fell.

Ashcombe's Jaguar rose up below me. I hit the roof hard, my knees buckling as a fresh new agony tore through my senses. Then pain burst through my torso as I dragged myself off the dented roof and fell sharply to the ground.

I yelled out. It felt like a thousand invisible needles stabbed at my nerves as I pulled myself up and hobbled away. Fresh tinkles of glass fell behind me. I turned back to see the assassin standing in the room above, framed by the shattered window. It stared down at me before turning away.

I staggered into the cover of the forest, half running, half limping, my body a map of hurt. Hellwyn's last, dying gaze played through my mind as if it were on a torturous loop. I ached to turn back and slay that bastard Prentice and the assassin, to burn the house down around them, but I knew in that instance I was beat.

I wasn't giving up. No, I was going after them, but on my terms.

I waited among the trees, watching the house as I waited for the assassin to leave and for Prentice to be on his own. I was looking forward to ending the bastard's life, but only once he'd given up the whereabouts of whoever was controlling the Hexling

It was a simple enough plan.

White hot agony continued to roar through my body. I reached into my bag for a vial of narcspyce. It would deaden the pain, as well as my senses for a short while, but that was a risk I was willing to take.

Soon, the discomfort receded and as it did, it was replaced with grief and horror. The trees blurred around me as realizations filled my thoughts and tears of fury stung my eyes.

Despite spending only a short time with Hellwyn, I'd grown to like her. She was powerful, admirable. Maybe we would have grown to be allies, God knew I needed some. But she was gone now and I felt as if at least some of her blood was on my hands. She'd successfully evaded the assassin and Prentice during their spate of murders. But then I'd blundered into her life. She'd counted on me to help and I'd let her down. And now she was dead.

Just like Tom.

I slid down the tree and sprawled across the cold ground, anger and sorrow chasing each other's tails as I stared at the distant house and swore I'd end Prentice, the Hexling, and its master before the day was out.

- FORTY ONE -

After a time Prentice left the house, alone. He frowned as he inspected the roof of the Jaguar, before climbing inside. I forced myself to my feet. The pain was bad, but I'd had worse. I stumbled through the trees as the car rolled down the drive.

The motorbike was exactly where I'd left it. I rooted through my bag. I had three crystals left, and my ammo was severely depleted. I considered calling Underwood, but what was the point? He'd warned me to back off, to let the Organization deal with it. No, I was on my own.

As ever.

I grasped the crystal tightly, drained its power and used it to tail the Jag. Its silvery trail was still visible. Just. I grabbed the helmet, dusted it off, turned the motorbike on and held my breath as it rumbled into life.

The wheels skidded through the wet leaves as I jumped down the incline and landed squarely in the middle of the dirt road. The silver lines of the Jaguar still threaded through the air, but were fading fast.

I gunned the engine and swept down the hill to where the silver trails grew brighter. Once I saw the car's tail lights I fell back, eager not to get spotted. The car roared down the highway as the heavens opened up and rain pounded the pavement. I kept back and put a few cars between us, my mood calm and focused, until he turned off toward the hills.

The hills that housed the asylum.

The sky darkened and the rain continued to fall cold and hard. I merged off the highway, following the Jaguar as it wound its way up that horribly familiar road, toward the wooded summit and the dark place that inspired my nightmares.

I ditched the motorbike near the gates and cut through the thick forest near the top of the hill. Pain still wracked my body and I was tempted to down another vial of narcospyce, but I needed to keep my head clear.

My senses were hyper alert; it felt like I could see every blade of grass leaning in the breeze. As I stumbled up a slope of muddy earth and glistening roots, I glanced back to see the highway far below and in the distance, the city.

It seemed so very far away. An entire world away.

I reached the summit and paused to catch my breath and load my gun. Cold rain fell upon my face like a baptism. I lifted my head to the billowy charcoal sky, loosened the catch on my scabbard and looked back to the great dark building nestled in the trees.

That black and broken place, that factory of nightmares and utter dread.

The place hadn't changed, repressive brownstone blocks, barred windows and the towers strangled in ivy. The stony drive sat empty but for the silver Jaguar with the dented roof.

I stuck to the tree line and made my way around the back of the building, hoping to find a way in without being detected. My heart raced. It felt like the very air itself pulsed with foreboding and the heavy aura of evil and suffering weighed on me. It emanated from the asylum, seeping though the invisible blanket of despair that covered it like a shroud.

There was magic here. Deep magic. It welled up from unspeakable sources. I thought back to the tunnel in the Hinterlands and my encounter with the werewolf and those black forces that had stirred inside me.

I never wanted to encounter anything like it again. It had saved my ass, but at what price? Proceeding now could likely put me in the same position again. Was I prepared to sacrifice my very being to that hideous darkness?

Again, I thought of calling the Organization. They were equipped to deal with situations like this. They could send in more experienced agents, even if they were little more than bounty hunters. The problem was I couldn't trust them, not with this; it was too close to home. I had to be the one to avenge Hellwyn and Tom and I needed to know, with all certainty, that justice had been done.

I ran alongside the back wall of the building and finally found a broken window, a few dagger-like shards of glass jutted from the frame. I smashed them out, climbed up to the sill and dropped in, landing on a hard floor peppered with broken glass.

The room was vast, its soot-stained ceiling high and wide. It reeked of decay and piss but the checkered linoleum floor still held a faint tang of antiseptic, a ghostly scent from the past.

I could feel the despair and almost hear the cries and screams of the poor tormented souls who had been committed here. The air stirred around me, as if the shades of yesterday were still shuffling through the rooms. Dead now, their lost souls forever roaming the place of their torment.

Being back made me feel sick. I despised the place, loathed the sight of its cracked walls and the stench of madness and distress. I'd vowed never to come back. And here I was, like a fly choosing to revisit the spider's web.

Gruff laughter echoed down the dark corridor beyond; I stole across the room and peered round the charred, broken door.

The long hall was bathed in gloom despite the candles that were dotted along the length of the floor. The flames flickered within the thick waxy stumps. Some yellow and orange, some electric-blue.

Witch fire.

I slipped into the shadows as a figure appeared at the end of the corridor. It was huge and definitely not human. Its hair seemed to writhe and dance as it turned and kicked a door open, stepped through, and slammed it shut.

Voices chattered, whispered and gibbered as I inched along the hallway.

The asylum was full once more, but now it seemed the inmates had been replaced by squatters. Dark magic filled the air. I caught glimpses of demons, gaunt-faced magicians and heavy-set trolls.

I reached into my bag and pulled out my penultimate crystal and clutched it hard, allowing its magic to soak through me. I conjured a simple cloaking spell to hide myself from view. If any of them looked my way, they'd see one of their own, but with a face full of boils and sores - something to stay away from.

The spell worked as I passed a pair of vampires. They backed against the wall, their lips curling with disgust. I continued on. The place was swarming with Nightkind. There was no telling how many had gathered below the asylum's roof, or exactly what had attracted them. Was this where the darkness smothering the city was originating from?

I thought of the black portal, that dark star of my visions, and wondered if it was still upstairs. Yes it was, I could almost hear its heavy ocean-like hum.

Blood spattered glass, clear and red, crunched below my feet as I walked towards the great staircase ahead.

Someone was descending.

A woman.... She was grey within the murk, as if she'd been woven from shadows. Long black hair fell down her back.

It could be anyone.

My heart pounded hard.

But she looked like Elsbeth Wyght. *A lot* like Elsbeth Wyght.

I pulled out my gun, my hand shaking violently.

One shot was all it would take.

She stepped into the hallway, her long off-white dress trailing to the ground. Someone walked with her, a powerful looking woman with rich golden hair twisted into a bun. The pair of them headed toward the front doors.

I stalked after them, my hand tightening on the gun's grip.

It was a clean shot. She'd be dead before she could even think of counteracting my attack. But what if it wasn't her? The gunfire would alert every creature in the place to my presence.

Indecision crippled me as I watched the two women approach the door. The blonde reached out and held it open for the woman in the dress. Daylight burst through the doorway, melting the details of the dark-haired woman into a silhouette.

My feet were frozen. My heart screamed to go after them, while my head told me to holster the gun and finish the job I'd started.

And then the doors slammed shut, the light vanished, and they were gone.

I felt sick. I forced myself to take a deep breath as I began to climb the wide stairway. The wooden steps felt solemn and heavy, or maybe it was the memories the place was bringing to mind. I hadn't climbed these stairs in years and somehow it felt like I was ascending toward the end.

Figures shifted in the darkness around me. Eyes glowed and voices rasped. I ignored them, kept my head down, and stepped onto the landing as I made my way along the corridor ahead.

Nausea flooded through me but I continued step after step.

The hairs on my neck prickled. Someone was following me. I could smell blood and mania as I counted their thumping, slapping predatory paces.

My hand strayed to my gun but I left it in its holster. It would be too loud.

I unsheathed my sword and whirled around.

- FORTY TWO -

A demon prowled behind me. A wild, crazed thing with scales like carbon-black diamonds protruding from its head. Its eyes were silvery gashes and it grinned, revealing short, sharp thickset teeth as it lunged.

Kill.

I swung the sword with a two-fisted grip and slashed the demon's throat. It gasped, the sound almost comical. I grabbed it by its lumpy head and pulled it back into a small room with a barred window and a cracked porcelain sink. The demon was dead and by the time I dumped it in the corner, its skin was already turning to ash.

I slipped out the door and carried on down the long dark hall, my heart thumping madly.

Cells lined the walls on both sides. Most of the doorways were open and I passed them in a dream-like trance until I heard a whimper in a windowless cell lit by smoking tallow candles stacked upon an old wheelchair.

A dark eyed boy, barely a teenager, sat in the corner. He gazed back at me while an ancient, hunchbacked vampire leaned over him, his forearm gently cradled in its gnarled hand. It would have been an almost tender gesture if the creature hadn't had its mouth clamped over the boy's wrist.

A trickle of blood ran from the vampire's pallid lips and down its wrinkled chin.

I didn't hesitate and was almost upon the parasite when the boy moaned, his glassy eyes widening as they focused on me.

The vampire turned, its pinched feral face as pale as porcelain in the gloom. Then its yellow eyes flashed as it stared into my eyes and hissed, baring long curved fangs.

Before the creature could move, I leaped forward and drove the sword through its heart. It opened its mouth to cry out but I clamped it shut with my hand. A dangerous move.

The vampire twitched and as the light dimmed in its eyes, I withdrew my hand and pulled the blade from its chest. The boy whimpered as I cut the duct tape that bound his ankles.

I reached into my bag for salve and a length of bandage to wrap around the wound on his wrist. "You need to get out of here," I whispered. "Can you do that?"

He shook his head, his face filled with terror.

"Yes you can," I said as I grabbed him and made him look into my eyes. "You have to. Now go, and be silent."

I watched as he crept away, sluggish and confused. He made it to the stairs and then vanished from view.

There were more cells, stretching to the end of the corridor, and by the sounds drifting out from them, this was not an isolated incident. But I couldn't clean this up on my own. There was a more pressing issue to be dealt with and I needed to get it done quickly. I'd have to return for these monsters and their livestock after I'd found Prentice.

If there was an afterwards.

A few candles flickered along the hall that yawned before me but it was a dark stretch nonetheless. Even with my bag of tricks, my gun and my sword, I felt woefully unarmed. And unprepared. Devilry oozed around me and magic thrummed within the walls, tempting me with its dark force. I ignored its call and carried on toward a crossroads, my heartbeat hard and loud.

An offshoot. Another corridor. One I remembered with every inch of my being. The cracked green paint, the scuff marks, the dents in the wooden floor. It was like a mausoleum to the past, every horrific feature intact.

Two figures lingered by the double doors, an ogress and a tall man who seemed to be missing half his face. I strode towards them with a confidence I didn't feel, stopping as they stepped from the shadows and barred my way.

The ogress held a length of pipe, the man a machete.

There was no way around, so I'd have to go through them.

The man looked to be the quickest, lean and spry, he'd have to go first. I grinned and beckoned to him. As I pulled my sword from its sheath he gritted his teeth and swung the machete. I danced aside and put my blade swiftly through his side, right up to the hilt.

His machete hit the floor with a heavy clunk.

I had no time to recover my sword before the ogress charged. I pulled my gun from its holster and fired. The shot echoed down the hall. She fell to her knees, and toppled to her face with a solid thump.

So much for being covert.

Howls and cries echoed through the building.

This was it, no more time. I seized the double doors, threw them open and stepped inside.

The room was long and dimly lit but for a single square of bright light that fell upon the bare floorboards from the skylight above.

And on the far wall.

The painting.

From here it looked to be at least ten feet tall, an immense block that swirled in a constant flux of charcoal black and midnight blue. Splatters of paint flecked the wall around it, giving the impression that it had been rendered with insane abandon. One indication, perhaps, of the desperate broken minds that must have created the abomination.

Looking upon it was like a punch to the gut. The portal, was real.

Two men stood below it. They'd clearly been in deep conversation before I'd entered the room, now their attention had turned to me.

One was Prentice Sykes. His hand strayed into his coat as he glared at me.

The other was a ghostly shadow of a man. A shade.

He wore a merlot-colored frock coat and a dingy white frilled shirt. Raven black hair fell to his shoulders, framing his long pale face and the shadows that pooled in his eyes as he regarded me. He looked like the ghost of a poet, some demented, addled spirit from another century. A phantom with one foot in this world and the other in some distant dimension.

A walker between worlds.

Like me.

A pang of horror crept across my flesh.

Was this the man Lyra Fitz had dreamt of? The gatherer of shadows...the black force that smashed the planets to dust?

The shade drifted towards me, stopping short of the square of light upon the floor. He nodded. "And you are?" His voice was soft and well spoken.

"Morgan Rook. And I'm here to kill you, although it looks like someone's already done most of the job for me."

"I'll deal with him." Prentice Sykes pulled his sword from its sheath. The shade turned to him and whispered. Prentice lowered the blade and regarded me with a sardonic smile. "My name is Rowan Stroud. I have a feeling we've met before. Where-"

"Why did you kill them?" I bolted forwards and stood in the center of the light.

"Kill who?" Stroud asked.

"Tom and Hellwyn."

He glanced back to Prentice, and then to a side door I'd failed to note. Was the assassin lying in wait? Did this ghost need protection?

"Why did I kill them..." Stroud placed a finger on his chin and his eyes gleamed as he glanced back at me. "Vengeance. Their cards were marked the moment they killed me and slaughtered everyone I ever loved."

"You're the cultist-"

"Cultist? I suppose a lesser mind might describe me thus. Who told you our story? Tom? Hellwyn?" He cocked his head and stared at me, as if trying to work out what I was.

"You should've stayed in your grave." I brought my sword up and advanced but the shade drifted back towards the painting.

"Oh. The cowardly knight versus the man with the hand-me-down sword. How will it end?" His laugh was short and cruel. I had no idea how to kill a shade but I was looking forward to finding out.

Prentice raised his blade and walked towards me. I backed out of the sunlight, hoping to draw him in. The moment the light hit his eyes, I'd decapitate the son of a bitch.

Stroud clapped his hands. The ghostly boom took me by surprise as it echoed like distant thunderclaps. "No. This is not how it's meant to be."

Prentice turned back. "I can do this."

"No, you can't. You're a spent force, Prentice. But you've helped me wipe out the Order, so at least you can depart this world with a smidge of redemption."

"We had an agreement," Prentice said, his voice rising.

"I never agreed to anything," Stroud turned to me. "You asked why your friends died and the simple truth is it happened because Prentice Sykes wanted to be free of the nasty little tumor in his gut. Their lives for his, that was his offer. He brought me to this world because he thought I'd be desperate enough to serve him. He was wrong. Wrong, wrong, wrong."

Anger flashed in Prentice's eyes. He stopped just short of the light as he turned back. "You would never have found this world if it wasn't for me-"

"You expect gratitude? Loyalty? After what you did? A fury crept into Stroud's voice. "I'm afraid it's out with the old order, and in with the new. However, I will give you a fitting send off. Snakes for the snake."

Tendrils of black smoke oozed from the painting and drifted into Stroud's form. His eyes grew bright and he held his hands out, drawing shadows from every corner of the room.

The gatherer of shadows.

The tendrils shifted and began to flow from his palms. They writhed in long coils, snakes formed of darkness, with amber eyes and madly flicking tongues.

Prentice turned ashen.

"That's right," Stroud said. "You're not fond of snakes, are you?"

They slithered over the floor with a sound like a thousand whispers, their bodies thick and swollen. Prentice backed towards the light, oblivious to me, as each snake became intent upon him.

He stood in the light and held his sword before him, preparing for them to strike but they stopped at the edge of the square and hissed.

"Fuck you!" Prentice said. There was a haughty note of triumph in his voice.

I could have shoved him back into the shadows, but I didn't. No, I wanted to fight the son of a bitch myself.

Stroud raised a hand to the skylight and whispered.

The glass blackened until the light grew dim enough for the snakes to breach it. They lunged towards Prentice and slithered up his legs as he screamed and hacked and slashed. His panic betrayed him as he cut both the snakes and himself. Blood sprayed from the gashes in his legs, sending the snakes into a frenzy. Their bodies swelled as they began to encompass his flailing form.

His scream was cut short when a fat swollen snake coiled across his head, encircling his mouth, then his nose. His eyes grew wide and he began to flail madly.

I almost ran to help him. Almost. Instead I watched in horror as the creatures writhed around him and he collapsed under their spectral weight.

The snakes struck, their teeth long and sharp as they punctured his exposed flesh. Smoke rose from the wounds, his skin began to char and the snakes slithered in a frenzy until I could see nothing but a writhing mass of black.

Soon silence fell over the room as the snakes slithered back into the shadows, leaving a pile of charred bones upon the floor.

"The Order is no more," Stroud said. "I'd expected to feel a greater sense of satisfaction but in truth, it's been quite the anticlimax. Perhaps it's because I've encountered a new problem, and it's in need of a solution. Tell me, who are you?"

"I gave you my name."

"But it isn't really yours, is it? You weren't born in this world. Tell me, how did you come to arrive here?"

"I was born right here, in this room." I walked towards him, my heart beating hard, fear battling to offset my raging fury and loathing.

"The portal? It only links this world with my own..." He gazed back at the canvas. I raised my sword, spurred by the glint of its light in the gloom.

I had no idea if it would harm him, but there was only one way to find out.

Stroud turned back to me. "You're not going to give up, are you?"

"No. I'm going to annihilate you. First you, and then your assassin."

"Really? Why wait then, let me summon it for you." Stroud gestured to the door as it flew open.

- FORTY THREE -

The assassin burst into the room, its eyes gleaming, dead and blue behind its mask. It glanced to Stroud, awaiting his command. He nodded and the unspoken order passed between them. I didn't need to hear it to know what it was.

With several leaps I sprang back toward the far end of the room hoping to buy myself a few scant moments. Time after time I'd seen what this creature could do. It seemed unstoppable, that to fight it would bring nothing but death.

But now wasn't the time for fear. Now was the time for vengeance.

My sword glimmered, its blade brimming with power as it awaited my intent. I itched to run forward, to meet the creature and hack at it with all the power I could muster.

Instead I watched as the assassin prowled towards me, the tip of its blade scraping and gouging the floorboards. Behind it, Stroud watched, his form thin and dark but for his softly glowing eyes.

His evil, remorseless arrogance filled me with rage and disgust. If I just could get to him...

The assassin brought its sword up two handed.

This was going to hurt.

I parried, wincing as the familiar shockwave of pain shot through my wrists and arms. The assassin brought its sword up for another swing. I lunged forward, testing its defense. It brought its blade across its chest to counter the blow.

I swung again.

It matched my maneuver.

Again and again. The same defense. The same attack. Hellwyn would have spotted this pattern if she'd had the chance. Tom too if he hadn't given up.

I focused my intent and allowed it to flow through me, from mind to blade.

The sword thrummed as if in accord.

I stepped back as the assassin brought its weapon up and swung, its blade a silver arc descending towards me.

I blocked it.

It was all I could do to hang onto the hilt as the blow juddered through my arm. I jumped back and sidestepped its next attack.

The assassin's sword smashed into the hardwood floor and stuck.

I lunged.

Time seemed to slow as the assassin furiously wrenched its sword free and brought it up to parry my blow. I changed course and the tip of my blade sliced through the assassin's arm, cleaving its hand off.

Its sword clattered to the ground. The hand spasmed, leaped like a spider and scuttled towards the fallen blade as acrid black wisps of smoke spilled from the wound.

It made no sound as it swept down to retrieve its sword.

Sever.

I waited for the assassin to seize the weapon before lopping off its other hand.

It lumbered back, smoke spilling from the stumps at the end

of its arms. And then it narrowed its eyes and it dropped its useless limbs, as if resigned to the killing blow.

"And...now...your...head," I growled, fury and adrenaline coursing through me.

The assassin closed its eyes, anticipating a blow that never came as I flew past it, my sights locked on Stroud.

-FORTY FOUR -

"I'm impressed," Stroud said. "My Hexling was skilled. It decimated highly trained knights and-"

"It was predictable," I said. "But most of the people you ambushed with it didn't see it coming. I did."

"Clearly there's more to you than meets the eye." Stroud held his hands out, coaxing the shadows back towards him. They formed a black, swirling pool at his feet. "I've only been in this world a short time, but I've seen considerable evidence of the fragile mental stamina this place inspires. I see it in you too." He closed his eyes and clapped his hands.

The dark pool shifted and three black columns rose up. They formed bodies with defined torsos, arms, legs and heads. Shadows swirled around them, refining their features as sparks ignited in their eyes.

My heart ached when the recognition took hold.

Tom, Hellwyn...

and Willow.

The venomous expression on her face was like a sucker-punch.

Tom was the first to strike. The sword had been formed from shadow, but it cut like a razor. The slash in my thigh would have been deeper if I hadn't jumped back. It smarted as if the blade had been laced with acid and salt.

I barely had time to move as Hellwyn lunged forward. Her sword struck the sleeve of my coat as I pulled away. Tom leaped forward, his sword sweeping in a black arc towards me. I ducked as it sliced through the air above my head.

Tom's shadowy form was thrown off balance. I stepped forward and drove my sword through his throat. Dark drops of matter misted the air. Tom clamped his hand over the wound but the inky blood continued to flow. The shadow creature swayed on its feet and the lights in its eyes began to dim as the phantom unraveled to nothing.

Hellwyn's sword rushed towards me.

"Block!" I fell back and hit the floor hard, my sword deflecting the majority of the blow as I scrambled back to my feet and a second figure closed in.

Willow.

Her sword grazed my hip as I rolled to the ground amid a shower of sparks. Then both Willow and Hellwyn came at me as one.

I dropped to my knee and parried Hellwyn's blade.

"End!" My sword arced back, passed through her midriff and she burst into slivers of shadowy smoke.

Willow's sword came from nowhere. I managed to block the brunt of the blow but the tip slashed the back of my hand, opening a gash in my flesh. I cried out in agony as my arm spasmed. It felt like a stream of icy fire had been injected into my veins.

I crumpled, barely countering her second and third strike.

She brought her blade up for a final stroke, leaving herself wide.

I fell forward and drove my sword through her heart.

She shuddered, her eyes wide.

Her look of anguish made me sick to my core and it was all I could do to keep myself together. "She's not real," I whispered. "She's-"

The agony of my wounds raged and a fresh wave of nausea passed through me. Like a deep black contagion had seeped into my veins and was slithering toward my heart.

Willow's shadow form began to fade, the betrayal on her fleeting face the deepest wound of all.

I climbed to my feet, fury coursing through me as I charged toward Stroud. He watched, his face impassive. "Where did you learn to fight like that?" he asked.

I had no words. I brought up my blade as one intention passed through my mind.

Stroud shook his head. "It's a pity to see such a talent go to waste, but clearly there's no other choice." He closed his eyes and raised his hands, as if intending to bring the ceiling down upon our heads. The last of the shadows snaked towards him and the room became impossibly bright as he opened his mouth to swallow them. His skin turned from ashen to coal and his eye sockets filled with pools of darkness, as if the shadows had consumed him from the inside out.

He thrust his hands out.

With the roaring crash of a tsunami, two black tentacles shot towards me, their barbed tips aimed at my heart.

There was nowhere to escape, no defense.

I closed my eyes and opened my soul to the deep magic buzzing through the asylum. It thrummed up through the floor and filled me with a heady rush.

The shadows continued to thunder towards me. I let them. As they smashed into me, it was all I could do to stand against them. Then my whole body convulsed with the raw and terrible force.

I opened my mouth to release the crescendo of power building inside me and my cry became a hungry, primal roar.

Images flashed through my mind, terrible vignettes of pain, squalor and despair. Echoes of the patients who'd lived and died in this terrible place bound within the darkness and festering energy Stroud had been feeding off.

When I opened my eyes I saw the world through a filter of unfettered fury and hatred. I rushed towards Stroud. He glanced toward the door as if seeking help. I threw out a command, it smashed shut and dust drifted like snow from above.

Stroud backed towards the painting. I conjured a ball of jet black flames in my hand and let it fly as he stepped back into the portal. It burst across its surface, turning it fiery red as the flames danced across the canvas.

A voice cried out. I couldn't understand the words, but they were Stroud's. He glared back at me as his ghostly face began to merge with the flames. And then he was gone.

The fire roared, illuminating the boiling swirls and ridges of black paint. Faint figures were tossed within its dark waves, the artists who had somehow been coaxed to paint out their despair, madness and torment. And in doing so, had opened a portal between worlds.

I strode from the room as it filled with the caustic fumes, and my body surged with malevolent black intent.

-FORTY-FIVE-

The magic seethed through me as I stalked down the corridor. It whispered, cajoling me to do terrible things. Slash, burn and maim. To smash anyone I encountered into dust.

It was impossible to defy the urges as they raged, demanding violent resolution. They rooted deep within me like a black pestilence and the terror I'd once had for this place was long gone.

I had no fear now.

I *was* fear.

Nightkind wandered from the cells and feeding rooms. They stood before me and howled with defiant fury and despicable threats.

I met their eyes.

And they began to cower.

They'd shown no mercy to their victims, to those vulnerable wretched figures still cowering and crippled in the cells. So I'd show the tormentors no mercy either.

Two hulking wolf men rushed at me.

The power surged through me as I punched through the chest of the first and squeezed its pulsing heart into pulp. My hand was wet as I pulled it out and threw the creature against the wall.

I drew my sword, beheaded the other and kicked its twitching corpse to the floor.

The rest began to flee. I grabbed one, a demon with an ancient, wicked face.

"Please!" it begged.

It tried to squirm free but I held it tight and stared into its eyes. "Who was he?"

"Who?" I could almost see the thoughts racing through its wicked mind and the lies it was desperately constructing.

I placed my palm on its forehead until it screamed. "And you think you're evil." I grinned as I pressed my hand harder. Its knees buckled and it almost dropped to the floor. I grabbed the fiend by the shoulders and smashed it into the wall. "Tell me who he was or I'll fucking eviscerate you." *This isn't you,* a thought whispered. But it didn't matter, because whoever I'd become, I was on the verge of getting an answer.

A strange expression passed through the demon's eyes as it gave me an almost beatific smile. "The walker?" he asked, his voice almost a whisper. "The shade in the shadows? A great, great force. The greatest force I've ever seen."

It spoke like a religious zealot. The irony of this wasn't lost on me.

"Tell me who he was."

The demon stopped struggling and went limp in my hand. "Do what thou wilt," it said with another serene grin, "shall be the whole of the law."

I broke its neck and dropped it to the ground. The others, having witnessed our exchange, turned and scattered.

I went after them, cutting them down one by one, spattering the cracked walls with their blood. Howls and screams broke out, shrieks of terror and pain. The walls seemed to shake with their cries, as if recalling familiar pleas from decades past.

I marched on, making my way through the bloody asylum. Consumed by a terrible black rage matched with an evil, eldritch force. Except it wasn't me. It was someone else. And I could only watch as this relentless dark stranger entered cell after cell and cut down the monstrous inhabitants within and gruffly freed the wretched humans stained by the gore of their abusers.

Panic swept through the asylum.

Many of the creatures fled.

Many died.

Soon, it was empty.

- FORTY SIX -

I stood before the doors, my sword dripping as I gave one last roar to force the rage and horror out. And then I threw the doors open and staggered into daylight.

The bright sun hit me hard and brought a fresh bout of nausea. I dropped my sword and leaned over as my body rejected the magic's black poison. Remnants of it still swirled through my system as I straightened up and wiped my mouth.

I reached into my bag, found a spent crystal and held it tight as I channeled the last of the abominable energy into it. Swirls of inky darkness passed from my hands, turning the clear shard a deep opaque black.

I'd need to find a safe place to dispose of it, somewhere far from this cursed, desolate place.

The mild September sunlight felt almost blinding. I pulled out a pair of shades and slipped them on.

The woods surrounding the building were still, the creatures that had fled the asylum, long gone. A few straggled, broken people emerged from the building, their eyes wild, their faces lost. I'd need to call this in. I dialed Underwood and gave him a heavily edited rundown. He sounded dubious, but that was a problem for some other day. Next I called Dauple, who could barely contain his excitement.

Ashcombe's dented Jag gleamed upon the drive as I staggered on. I placed my hand over the keyhole and the door clicked open.

I climbed in, started the engine, and never looked back.

- FORTY SEVEN -

I hobbled up the stairs one at a time, my body aching, my head numb. I'd hoped to get to my apartment unscathed, but Mrs. Fitz was at the ready, her hand on her hip.

She took one look at my face, nodded politely and closed her door.

The second I stumbled into my apartment, I stripped off and threw my clothes into a black trash bag. They couldn't have been washed, but even if they had come clean I never wanted to see them again. The coat was a different matter. And I wondered if there was a dry cleaners that specialized in magical armor. One that didn't ask questions about blood, especially when it came in odd colors.

I took a hot shower and filled the room with steam. Then I sat on the edge of the bath and stared at the tile floor, before staggering back to the shower and scrubbing down all over again. Only then did I feel halfway clean.

The bed seemed to swallow me up as I fell upon it and passed out.

. . .

I awoke from what felt like a year's worth of bad dreams. Each had taken me back to the asylum where I'd found myself gliding down the corridors, bombarded by the screams of agony and delight coming from the cells.

Every route had taken me to the same end; the room with the painting.

No matter how hard I ran, the portal pulled me in, swallowing me up into the deep swirling abyss.

Each immersion into the canvas had been witnessed. People surrounded me as if standing before an exhibit. Many of the witnesses were from my past; my foster father, his bitch of a girlfriend, Tom, Hellwyn, Underwood and Willow. And there were others I didn't recognize. They'd gathered to see the monster, the beast Morgan Rook. I watched too, as if through the lens of an all seeing eye, and recoiled as my face split with sadistic evil.

I rampaged, sword in hand, cutting the witnesses down one by one and sending endless streams of blood washing over the floorboards.

The *other me*, my dark self, clapped his hands. It made no sound in this world, but I was sure it had been heard in some other realm.

As I got out of bed the dreams continued to swirl through my head but as I stood, my body exploded with pain, and the imagery ceased.

I stumbled through to the living room, made coffee and slumped onto the sofa, nestling the cup in my hands and absorbing the scalding heat.

I checked my phone. A message from Glory was awaiting my reply.

Tom's funeral was taking place this afternoon. Somehow I'd lost a whole day.

I sat back, contemplating the black coffee lapping against the side of the white cup. I wondered if I'd ever know who the shade Rowan Stroud really was, and whether or not I'd ever find him. More unfinished business, like Elsbeth Wyght. Two monsters, waiting to be slain. Someday.

I glanced up at Willow's photograph. "I think I nearly had her," I said. "Nearly." I gazed at her wild eyes and her soft kind smile. "Next time. I swear it."

A heavy darkness fell over me. I was too tired to fight it.

I sat and stared at the carpet until a fat, powder-blue Persian cat called Ash dropped in and padded across the floor. He jumped up beside me, his yellow-orange eyes wide as he gazed up and cried. I lifted a leaden hand to pet him and he purred like a muffled engine.

A Siamese slipped through the window next, along with her sister and two new cats with long black hair. They sat around me in a circle, staring.

It took me a moment to realize I was smiling. "Okay, I get it." I stood, stretched and went to the kitchen to fetch their breakfast. "No rest for the wicked."

. . .

I saw my reflection in a shop window, superimposed over fashionably dressed mannequins. The black suit and tie made a crisp contrast against my cream-white shirt. Dark grey clouds soared across the glass and a fat raindrop struck the sidewalk before me. I was so lost in my thoughts that I failed to notice the taxi that had pulled up, until the driver sounded his horn.

I looked up to see Underwood's violet eyes sparkling through the back window. He opened the door and nodded. "Get in, Morgan, I'll give you a ride. Where are you going?"

My voice sounded monotone as I named the cemetery. There was no point in rejecting his offer.

"Nice to see you in a suit." Underwood smiled. "But I'm very sorry for the occasion. The way things are going it seems likely we'll be attending many funerals over the coming months and years."

His eyes gleamed as he studied me. "You left quite a mess behind."

I glanced at the driver: a middle aged man with a thick beard and glassy eyes.

"Don't worry." Underwood said. "He won't remember either one of us, let alone our conversation. Tell me what happened at the asylum? Dauple said it was an out and out blood bath."

"I went and sorted out some problems, just like you told me not to." I matched his stare. "Someone had to do it."

"And do you care to explain how one man created such a scene?"

"I suppose we were both...misled about my abilities?" I matched his anger as the taxi crept through the traffic and thundering hail turned the world outside into a blur of white.

Underwood appeared to bite back his first response and slowly the fire in his eyes began to dim. "I knew you were gifted the moment I saw you. I also knew your power could go either way. For good or bad. I wanted you under the umbrella of the Organization. That way we could channel your gifts, use them for good. Or whatever passes for good these days."

"You should have trusted me."

He shook his head. "You were eighteen. Undisciplined. I loathe to think of the trouble you could have gotten into if you'd have realized your capabilities."

I shrugged. I could see his point but refused to concede it.

"Exactly. You'll never know, and neither will I. You were like a weapon, Morgan. I had to make sure you were secured, or that we were the ones to wield you."

"Who am I? And why-"

"When it comes to your past, I know about as much as you do. It's never interested me, it's irrelevant."

"My past's pretty relevant to me." I glanced outside. A young girl stared at me from the car in the next lane, her face indistinct through the hail-streaked window. I forced a smile. She returned it and waved, then turned back to her doll.

"My job was to turn you into an asset, that's all they asked me to do, nothing more. And maybe one day you'll thank your lucky stars." He sounded resigned."Fine. Do whatever has to be done. Dig up the past. Find out who you are, or who you were. But in the meantime we have work to do. And I need to know you're with me."

And what if I'm not, I wondered as I looked over at him. He smiled at me, but it didn't quite reach his eyes. I nodded. I was with him. For now at least. It was better to have the Organization behind me than standing in my way.

Underwood glanced at his cufflinks. They gleamed faultlessly. "Everything's changing, you don't need me to tell you that. But it means I'm going to need your *full* attention, Morgan. There are forces working against me. Elements..."

"In the Organization?"

He drew his lips into a line and glanced away. "Take some time off. Grieve. Recover. Recharge. Then come and see me. We need to discuss what happened, in detail. All right?"

"Sure."

Underwood had never really been this open with me before, so I decided to ask a question that had been bugging me for years. "Who runs the Organization?"

He smiled. "Who knows? I just follow orders. So should you."

The car pulled up to the curb. Graves stood in a row behind a high black iron railing. I got out to find the hail had subsided into hard cold rain.

I turned back to the car to see Underwood glance up at me, a strange expression in his lilac eyes. Hope? Fear? Or both?

Then the cab pulled away and he was gone.

- FORTY EIGHT -

I had no idea what I'd find at the funeral. All I knew was Glory said she'd be there, so at least there would be two of us.

The wind battered the rain at me as I walked along the stony path that ran between the graves. A large service was being held in the distance and I could see a black mass of mourners under their umbrellas. It was only when I caught a flash of Glory's signature red dress below her long black coat and hat, that I realized it was all for Tom.

I pulled my raincoat up to my neck and strode on, amazed at how many people were there. It was a mixed bunch; suited professionals, people he'd met on the streets and more than a few of the cagier members of the magical community. There was even an ogre, cloaked of course but obvious to my eyes.

Glory glanced up and nodded for me to join her. I nodded back and pushed my way through the starry eyed knot of men and women that had gathered around her.

An expensive marble headstone marked Tom's place in this unconsecrated part of the graveyard, and below it was a neatly dug hole and a polished mahogany coffin. Someone had lovingly paid good money to ensure he'd had a proper send off, and it was clear by the crowd standing below the slate-grey sky that Tom had been much loved and had walked in many different circles.

The realization made me feel hopeful somehow, and I smiled as Glory squeezed my hand, her eyes thankfully shielded below her thick black shades.

. . .

The wake was held in an ordinary bar. A mix of blues and contemporary folk blared from the speakers and the place heaved with people. There was food everywhere, not to mention a buffet crammed with hors d'oeuvres, casseroles, pastas, salads and a plethora of cakes. The bar was doing a brisk trade and after what seemed like forever, I managed to order myself a double whiskey.

Someone had cast a low level enchantment over the place so that the bar staff, and any other non-magical types, wouldn't quite notice the more unusual guests.

I had no wish to talk to anyone, so I stood by the window watching the rain pound the street. I lifted my glass. "To you, Tom, wherever you are." I swallowed the whiskey, enjoying the warm fiery blaze as it slipped down my throat.

The world seemed grayer than usual, which was fitting. As I thought of Tom, I thought of the assassin and the shade that had sent it. And I took a second vow. I had no idea how, but I would find Rowan Stroud, just like Id find Elsbeth Wyght.

Because that's what I did, I righted the wrongs as best I could.

"Can I buy you another?"

A blast of drug store aftershave filled my nostrils and I turned to find Dauple standing behind me, holding what looked like a glass of absinthe. "What are you doing here?"

He pulled a notebook from his coat and held it up. "I was in the graveyard minding my own business, and then I spotted you. Nice suit by the way."

Logging graves. Maybe. He did do that. "If I find out you followed me..."

Dauple looked insulted, and then angry. "I wasn't following you. But after I saw you leave the graveyard and come over the road to this fine establishment, I suppose maybe I did. Technically. But only to buy you a drink. You looked sad and soaked through. Like a puppy in a well."

"Listen, I appreciate the offer, but I need to be on my own for awhile. Process things, you know?"

Dauple nodded. "I know. So much to process. Death. Life. People. Flies. Traffic. More death." His eyes grew wide as he seemed to take in the gravity of his crazy thoughts.

"But...you know, I do have some business I need to take care of. And I could use some help, if you're free?" I needed to go back for Hellwyn, pay my respects and bury her but it really wasn't something I wanted to face alone.

"Indeed. I will always help you if you ask." Dauple's lips took on a slightly green tinge as he sank the rest of his absinthe.

"Thanks" I nodded and was about to walk away when Dauple reached out and grasped my wrist. Usually I'd have words for him, but the gesture was oddly comforting.

"It will be alright, you know, everything will be. I think." He released my wrist and nodded, before vanishing into the crowd.

I downed the last of the whiskey and turned to look for Glory in an attempt to be social, when my phone buzzed.

I considered turning it off, then a message flashed on the screen.

- D.H. I got a call that's right up your alley. Am at the scene now, looks pretty bad.

"Doesn't it always." An abandoned glass of beer rested on the table before me. I thought about dropping my phone in and taking that vacation I'd promised myself.

But I didn't.

Because as they say, there truly is no rest for the wicked.

THE END

MIDNIGHT FALLS

BOOK TWO OF THE ORDER OF SHADOWS IS AVAILABLE NOW

READ ON FOR A FREE PREVIEW

-CHAPTER ONE-

I liked going to The Rocket Bar; it wasn't in the city's magical quarter and *blinkereds* drank there. It was where I met my normal friends. They invited me to join them every Friday, despite my dismal track record for showing up. Not that it was personal, it was just hard to be reliable when your life revolved around hunting rogue vampire gangs, tracking vicious demons, and dealing with murderous banshees.

None of these friends knew about my secret life, or the other worlds that lurked just outside their view, and I hoped that it would stay like that for as long as possible. Things were easier that way.

"Hey, Morgan, we're switching to tequila. You in?" Marty asked. Marty was the unofficial ringleader of this group of reprobates and the one that had invited me to join their boozy fellowship.

"Sure!" I called across the table. Why not? I hadn't touched a drop since Dauple and I buried Hellwyn. That had only been about a week ago, but somehow it seemed like another lifetime, despite the bruises I still wore from those battles.

I sat back in the chair as the din of the bar pulsed around me. Marty and the others had been here for at least an hour judging by the number of empty glasses, and it seemed they'd already built up a good buzz. Them and their new recruit, the attractive, somewhat embittered woman sitting next to me. The one whose hand kept brushing my thigh. We'd only been introduced ten minutes ago, and I was struggling to remember her name.

"Seriously," she said, slurring her s's, "I loathe him."

Him being her manager. This was at least the third time she'd told me what a piece of shit he was. Her breath was laced with vodka and whatever mixer had turned her drink that bizarre shade of blue. I'd made the mistake of asking what she did for a living, and had since deleted the painfully intricate details of her accountancy job from my mind.

Her hand brushed my leg again. I ignored it. She wasn't my type.

I was about to plot my escape when she leaned in close for another salvo of sour-breathed monologue, "Seriously, I'm telling you, there's nothing worse than being under appreciated."

That much I could relate to. I'd never felt appreciated by my employers at the Organization either. I knew I wasn't as valued as their other agents, I was rarely kept in the loop and my salary was a joke. Still, it was a moot point, because as of last week I wasn't even sure if I still had a job. Erland Underwood, my eccentric part-Fae boss, had given me time off until *further notice*. I still hadn't heard a word from him.

"He's such a dick," the woman said again. Her eyes glinted in the candlelight as her hand rose further up my leg. "You know?"

Her emphasis on the word *dick* wasn't quite as subtle as she thought it was. I had to get away. Draw the line or end up ensnared in a mess I definitely wasn't drunk enough to even consider getting caught up in.

I looked over as Marty approached from the bar with a tray of tequila shots in his hands and a mischievous grin on his face. "Glad to see you two are hitting it off," he said, glancing from me to the mystery blonde.

"I-" My phone rattled. I grabbed it.

- Haskins - I've got a situation.

I was about to text my halfhearted reply when the phone began to rumble and the screen lit up with *Haskins* in big bold letters. "Excuse me," I said. My unwanted companion muttered and gave an irritable flick of her wrist as I walked toward the door.

The air outside held a brisk October chill. I stood under the bar's awning and watched an autumn-addled fly buzz in listless circles as I answered the phone. "Morgan."

"You gotta come right now!" Panic barbed Haskins' usually nonchalant voice.

"What's the problem?"

"There's something weird going on. Your type of weird. I need help!"

"I'm on leave, I'm unarmed, and frankly I'm not that interested." And I wasn't. This was the first break I'd had in longer than I cared to remember.

"Well you *should* be worried. People have gone missing. They could be hurt or worse. Get over here, Morgan."

I sighed. The weight of the last few weeks still bore down on me and my limbs still ached in a hundred different places. I watched as the fly committed suicide in a flickering zapper and exploded with a crackle and pop. "Fine. But you owe-"

"Hickory Street. Come quick."

"I'm on my way."

I ducked back into the bar to get my raincoat. Luckily it doubled as magical armor and I had a feeling I was going to need it.

"You're not going?" Marty asked, holding out a tequila.

"Sorry. I've got to. I'll be back if I can, but don't wait up." I dropped enough money to pay for a drink I hadn't even sipped and nodded to the blonde. It seemed she'd already forgotten who I was. I couldn't blame her.

I flagged a cab, sat in the backseat and watched the city pass by.

Hickory Street was a bland row of houses that straddled the line between gentility and poverty. I paid the driver, crossed the road and slipped past Detective Haskins' car. He looked pale and his usually spiky hair was limp, but his pebble-like eyes gleamed as he turned and saw me.

"What's going on?"

"Fucked up stuff," Haskins said with his usual colorful directness as he got out of his vehicle. "We got a call at the precinct from an old woman who reckons she knows where some of our missing persons have gone."

"Missing persons?"

Haskins gestured to the surrounding street. "Two families, a newly wed couple, and a widower. And that's just in the last month. All from within a square mile of where we're standing."

"Any leads?" I asked, even though I was fairly sure I already knew the answer.

"Not a single one. Not that I'm officially on the case. The old lady's call got diverted to me. The desk sergeant knows to send the weirder inquiries my way."

"Which you then pass on to me, for a profit."

"So?" Haskins shrugged. "We all do well from it."

"Some more than others. Look, I'm not paying for this. I'm not earning right now, which means you're not either. The only reason I came was out of the goodness of my heart. Remember that."

"Sure."

"Tell me about the call." I glanced back toward the house. It wasn't what I'd consider a nice place, but whoever owned it had made an effort. The lights were off, but that didn't necessarily mean no one was home.

Haskins' breath frosted the air. "At first I thought the old broad was nuts. She kept saying the same thing over and over, *the starving man did it."*

"Starving man?"

"Yeah, you'll like this. According to the old goat there's a man who only comes out after dark. Apparently he eats anything he can get his hands on. Rats, pigeons, mice, the butcher, the baker, and the candlestick maker for all I know. I told you it was weird shit."

"Anyone here?"

"No. I don't know. I knocked and..." Haskins shivered as we walked up to the porch. "You don't need to be a wizard to see something's wrong with this place and I'm sure as hell not going in on my own."

And it's something you clearly don't want your colleagues to know about, so you called on me. I leaned toward the small glass window in the door and caught a strong scent of cooking.

Meat, rare and bloody.

Pork?

No, long pig.

Long pig and...bitumen?

END OF PREVIEW

Thank you so much for reading Dark City. I really hope you enjoyed the book. For exclusive free offers, giveaways, updates & new releases please visit:

www.kithallows.com

ALSO BY KIT HALLOWS

How to Kill a Witch
Midnight Falls

CPSIA information can be obtained
at www.ICGtesting.com
Printed in the USA
BVOW06s1309220118
505978BV00001B/1/P